THE SPIDER:
WHEN THOUSANDS SLEPT IN HELL

MASTER OF MEN!

WHEN THOUSANDS SLEPT IN HELL

By Grant Stockbridge

POPULAR PUBLICATIONS • 2021

CHAPTER 1
NIGHT OF TERROR

"SUMATRA... SIAM... Ceylon... India—" Softly, the romance-laden names came from Nita van Sloan's lips, and her low, rich contralto voice endowed them with a wealth of feeling, heartfelt yearning, as her eyes rested on the square shoulders and strongly handsome face of Richard Wentworth, who sat beside her at the sedan's wheel.

Momentarily her glance flashed to the car's other occupant, lounging negligently in the rear seat. In his immaculate evening dress, Earl Saunders was almost a duplicate of Wentworth. Even his features, though lacking the forceful vitality of Wentworth's dynamic, flat-planed face, were startlingly similar.

Like Wentworth, Earl Saunders was of excellent family, born to wealth and luxury. Unlike his longtime friend and college chum, he chose to take full personal advantage of that good fortune. For him the world was an extremely pleasant place of continual, varied entertainment and enjoyment—a place to which personal danger and hardship were entirely foreign.

Earl Saunders lived the sort of life that *might* have been Richard Wentworth's, were it not that something in Wentworth's blood refused to let him stand by idly, while injustice struck and the helpless were trodden underfoot by those ruthless marauders whom the law was unable to overtake. Wentworth had chosen the constant peril of a one-man war against crime—ceaseless

Tied to chairs in the humble kitchen were

victims asleep—never to awaken again!

danger that hung overhead like a Damoclean sword whenever the Spider took up the challenge of society's enemies and stalked the highways and byways of the underworld on a self-appointed mission of vengeance.

"The Fiji Islands, the Celebes, Indo-China and picturesque Bali," Saunders chuckled. "We'll stop at them all—peaceful, languorous lands where men take life easy and gangsters and machine guns are unknown. Nearly a year of interesting travel and nothing to do but worry about dressing for dinner. Better

come along, Nita. Better help me convince Dick that the New York police force can hold things down for him while he's gone."

Nita glanced again at his indolent slouch, carefree, grinning face. Yearning clutched at her heart. She would not have had Richard Wentworth as purposeless as Earl Saunders, for she knew that for him idleness had no savor. Yet to get him away from New York for almost a year, to know that he was safe each night when darkness fell, to be certain that his life was not hanging in the balance each moment when he was out of her sight—was a heaven to which she almost despaired of ever attaining!

For three days Earl Saunders had been stopping with Wentworth while waiting in New York for the sailing of the luxury liner that was to take him on a world cruise. Since the hour of his arrival he had dangled this alluring bait in front of Nita, trying to persuade them to book passage with him.

Recently things had been unusually quiet. The lull in Wentworth's ceaseless warfare against crime had led her to hope against hope that his long crusade might at last be drawing to a close—that finally she might be on the threshold of the happy, peaceful home, the realization of her fondest dreams. To have a peaceful home like other women, with Dick at her side, children to make their happiness complete....

Those things might be hers if Dick could be lured by this cruise. Tonight, as the three had sat dining in a New Jersey nightclub, it almost seemed Wentworth was won over. Plain and unmistakable in the depths of his keen, blue-gray eyes, she had read the same hungry desire that gnawed at her own heart.

Instinctively, she had sensed that he was on the verge of capitulating....

NOW, AS the car sped along Riverside Drive, Wentworth caught Nita's lovely violet eyes upon him and his pulse beat faster. All too well he realized what was in her mind and heart. Only too gladly would he have rewarded that love and devotion with the consummation they deserved... could he have done so with a clear conscience.

But, even though the past few weeks' undisturbed calm had made him hope that the need for his services might be past, that at last the Spider might put away his ebon habiliments and fade into the darkness out of which he had come—even though the quiet peacefulness of this night seemed far removed from any hint of trouble—still, he could not shake off the presentiment of evil that obsessed him.

Upon more than one occasion Wentworth had owed his life to hunches of this sort, and tonight the whispering voice of his warning sixth sense was insistent, undeniable.

Was this a genuine premonition that would give him no peace—or was it his own restless spirit conjuring up an imaginary menace? Well did he realize the lure which crime-fighting held for him—the thrill of matching wits with ruthless killers who laughed scornfully at police efforts to cope with them. Well did he know the irresistible urge to don the black cape and hat and take the grim, avenging trail when helplessness cried aloud for the redress which the Spider alone could give.

In that moment, Richard Wentworth made his decision.

Too long he had been thinking only of himself—resolutely

blinding himself to Nita's sacrifices, taking all that she had to offer and giving nothing in return. Now it was Nita's turn—and no figment of his imagination must deprive her of it.

A few blocks farther down the Drive, he recalled, was the apartment hotel in which Joe Remington kept his quarters. Remington, head of the Peerless Travel Agency, was just the man to handle reservations on the *Migantic* and make all arrangements for the world cruise.

Wentworth cut the gas, as they approached the building.

"Lucky thing we came along the Drive." He turned to Saunders. "I just remembered an appointment here in the Brockton. It may take me half an hour or so. Suppose you go ahead with Nita, and I'll meet you later in the Stork Club."

Saunders clambered in behind the wheel and reached for the brake. Nita made no protest, but her eyes framed an unspoken question, a half-fear that in this, her moment of near triumph, Dick was again plunging into danger. Then the car was underway, and Wentworth was striding under the hotel canopy.

It may have been the queer, enigmatical look in Nita's eyes that caused Wentworth to pause on the threshold. He hesitated in the doorway, and his gaze followed the departing sedan... just as a powerful, dark-hued car swept down the Drive and rapidly closed the distance between it and the taillights of Earl Saunders' sedan.

To a casual observer, there would have been nothing significant about that speeding car. Its effect on Wentworth was electrical. The half-drawn blinds, the taut-faced driver crouched close over the wheel, the sudden burst of power with which the machine shot forward—all screamed an ominous warning, even before the two cars were abreast and the quiet of the night shattered by a terrific explosion!

PARALYZED WITH horror, Wentworth saw the lurid flash of that blast. His car seemingly leaped into the air, then, blown half-apart, careened wildly across the road and crashed into a tree, as the other machine again sped on its way. Enervating dread chained Wentworth there, held him momentarily helpless as he visualized what he would find in that crumpled wreckage... Then, legs that threatened to buckle beneath him were hurtling him toward the wrecked sedan.

Again the silence of the night was all-pervading, like the stillness of doom itself, after the thunderous reverberation of that fearful detonation. The *slap-slap* of his shoes upon the pavement hammered in his brain, seemed trying to drown out something else that he must hear—something he must not forget.

"Tony Morelli! Tony Morelli!" was that instinctive warning. It didn't stop.

The man's name dinned into his consciousness—Tony Morelli, well-known petty leader of the underworld. In that fleeting fraction of a second when the pursuing car flashed past him, Wentworth's photographic eyes had glimpsed the driver, identifying him instantly. Tony Morelli....

Now Wentworth was beside the ghastly ruin, tugging at a twisted door, yanking it open... to stare into the dark interior.

7

The light of an arc-lamp, streaming in balefully through the shattered windows, revealed the gruesome sight within—Earl Saunders' slumped body, horribly mangled, almost unrecognizable.

"Nita! Nita, darling!" tore from Wentworth's lips as he squeezed into the battered tonneau and groped for her in the stygian shadows.

And then he found her—flung into the rear of the car. She was terribly wounded, but she still lived.

Blood drenched her neck and shoulders, streaming down her arms, but her heart beat strongly, and a low moan gasped from her lips before she lapsed into unconsciousness. She must be gotten to a hospital at once. Wentworth summed up swiftly. Help would come swarming to the wreckage, in a few moments—willing hands to speed her to the best of medical attention as quickly as he, himself, could hope to accomplish it.

Meanwhile, she faced a danger even more terrible than that of her wounds—*danger from him!*

The cold-blooded killer had done this horrible thing, done it to wipe out Richard Wentworth. The utter callousness of the outrage was an index of the man's vicious recklessness... the appalling danger that would hang over Nita until Richard Wentworth was dead.

But he *was* dead already—he must be dead! That was her only salvation... to eliminate himself entirely.

QUICKLY, WENTWORTH decided. That poor corpse behind the shattered wheel could easily be made to pass for his own. Swiftly, his fingers ran through Saunders' pockets and removed every personal effect. These he replaced with a card-case, billfold and ring that would identify the corpse as Richard Wentworth. For an instant he clasped one of the mangled hands in his own, squeezed the broken fingers... and silently

vowed to that innocent victim that his murderer would not go unpunished.

The wail of oncoming police sirens warned Wentworth that he had not a second to spare. Barely in time, he squirmed out of the wreckage, darted across the walk and over the wall, diving to cover on the wooded hillside just as flashlights stabbed out and shouting voices commanded him to halt.

From two directions they closed in on him, systematically beating the bushes, searching for him with screaming lead whenever their probing lights caught a flash of his white shirt-front. Craftily, Wentworth played hide and seek with them, led them down the hillside and then doubled in his tracks, to pass them on the way back to the top. He could not leave until he knew that Nita was being taken care of. And now the moan of an ambulance siren told him help had arrived.

The ambulance, he saw, was from the Calvin Memorial Hospital, one of the best in the city. Nita was being lifted into it. Then, grim-faced and tight-lipped, Wentworth disappeared among the shrubbery, silently worked his way between the bushes, until, a block and a half further up the Drive, he stepped out of cover in time to hail a taxicab and direct the driver down a side street.

Even as he had been eluding the police, his mind had been busily planning....

He was dead. He *must* be dead—certain that there was no giveaway, or that no keenly watching eyes were able to detect the fraud. For this reason, he must be dead to all his friends, servants, even to Nita—everyone except for his physician, Dr. Rogers.

The physician could be depended upon to keep his secret. Obligated to Wentworth for favors that were invaluable, he would keep a closed mouth even if death itself were the price of his silence. Rogers would be his confidant only because Wentworth *had* to have reliable reports on Nita's condition.

While the cab waited, he stepped into a drugstore and got the physician on the phone, quickly outlined the situation.

"You are her personal physician, Doc," he concluded. "Get up there to the Calvin Memorial as fast as a cab can take you. You are in complete charge—retained by me before I was killed. *I* am dead—don't forget that. You haven't heard a word from me. I'll keep in touch with you, in case—in case I should be needed."

Rogers' reassurances and pledge of silence were still coming over the wire when Wentworth clicked the receiver back onto its hook and hurried out to the taxi. Already his flying thoughts were leaping ahead, laying a foundation for the swift and implacable vengeance this outrage demanded....

RICHARD WENTWORTH was dead—but the Spider still lived, and the Spider needed another personality. He must have certain means of circulating, unsuspected, among his fellow men. Terry Trimble was the answer to that problem—a young private detective who had been quite seriously injured while working with Wentworth some weeks before.

Last week, Trimble had come out of the hospital, and Wentworth had insisted on retaining him—so that he might order him to take an extended vacation in the Adirondacks and recuperate at the home of his parents. Terry Trimble—a man of about Wentworth's build, with a mop of carroty hair and a broad-featured Irish face—would not be difficult to impersonate. Wentworth knew the address of Trimble's apartment—even the hidden desk drawer in which the young detective kept his credentials.

Two blocks from the apartment building, Wentworth dismissed his cab and traveled the rest of the way on foot. Unobserved, he slipped into the entrance, used a skeleton key on the door and took the automatic elevator up to the third floor. In a few minutes he had picked the lock, was stepping into the apartment and switching on the lights.

A cabinet photograph of Trimble stood on the mantelpiece. With this propped up on the table in front of him, and his ever-present makeup kit spread out, Wentworth went to work. Gradually, the sensitive lines of his cultured face disappeared, gave way to the higher cheekbones, broader nose and wider mouth that were Terry Trimble's. The crisp black hair became chestnut, then a carroty red. Even the poise of Wentworth's flat-backed figure and powerful, athletic shoulders, seemed to change, become less conspicuous, as he slipped into one of Trimble's suits and regarded himself before a full-length mirror.

11

In no more than ten minutes Richard Wentworth had disappeared… to be replaced by a twin of Terry Trimble. With a nod of satisfaction, Wentworth turned away from the mirror. Now the Spider was ready to avenge the death of Earl Saunders and face the deadly menace that had almost blasted Nita to her grave!

CHAPTER 2
THE BECKONING FINGER

IMPATIENTLY WENTWORTH waited for the morning papers and accounts of his death. From an outside telephone he made contact with Dr. Rogers, before retiring, and was relieved to learn that, while badly injured, Nita was in no immediate danger. Back in Trimble's apartment, he tried to sleep. But his brain was working too feverishly, vainly seeking some clue to the motive for that unprovoked, murderous attack.

Within a few days, Nita and he would have been married, watching the skyline of New York fade into the distance as their ship headed for those romantic lands which, now, Earl Saunders would never see again. On the verge of happiness had come swift disaster. Hot blood pounded through Wentworth's veins as he accepted the challenge.

With a pang of regret, he realized that the ways of peace, natural to other men of his culture and breeding, were not for him. So long as murderous beasts could operate in the world's greatest city, there was no ease and luxury for him—no laying aside of the grim Nemesis role which was the only force that these social pariahs feared.

The morning papers featured the story of his death—from the tabloids, with their gruesome photographs of his mangled body, to the more conservative journals with their second-page accounts of the tragedy and reviews of his career as dilettante criminologist. In all, the details were meager—simply that his car had been bombed by a man who apparently had waited for it at a lonesome point on the Drive and then made his escape toward the river before the police could apprehend him. There were the usual promises of prompt developments from the police, a shocked statement from Wentworth's friend, Commissioner Stanley Kirkpatrick, but nothing of value—until he came across an account, in one of the early afternoon papers, that linked up his own murder with the rather bizarre death of Willis Fleming, one of Wentworth's acquaintances.

Willis Fleming, it seemed, had been discovered dead in his bed when his valet had been unable to rouse him. There was no apparent cause of unnatural death or anything suspicious except a framed etching that hung on the wall directly in front of him—a shadowy figure of Death with hand outstretched, bony forefinger beckoning to the sleeper.

Even though Fleming's valet was certain that the curious picture had not been there the day before, no significance might have been attached to its presence except that a print of the same etching had been found in the room of Arnold Trautman, a wealthy importer, who had also died in his sleep three nights ago. The writer had been quick to pounce upon this circumstance and play it up—then link Fleming's death with Wentworth's when he discovered that Fleming had tried several times, the previous night, to contact Wentworth on the telephone.

"Mr. Fleming seemed to be very nervous and excited," Jackson, Wentworth's chauffeur and right-hand man, had reported to the police. "He called four times and wanted Mr. Wentworth to call him back as soon as he came in. The last time he kept saying, 'I've *got* to see him—tell him I've *got* to see him!'"

That was the only unusual circumstance Jackson could recall that had occurred during the evening—and the only possible reason he could ascribe for the attack which had resulted in Wentworth's death.

The only possible reason he could ascribe... But as Wentworth read that statement he could almost read Jackson's mind; visualize the scene in his Sutton Place stronghold, where Jackson would be conferring with huge, bearded Ram Singh, his personal man, and old Jenkyns, his butler. Those loyal followers, who were far more than servants to him, knew how to keep their own counsel. But Wentworth knew how they would be raking their memories for every possible suspect who might have accomplished his death.

He wished that he might call Jackson and his servants into his confidence, but that offered too much to risk. They would be watched, spied upon continually, if the man who had ordered his murder had the slightest doubt about his being dead. The merest slip, the barest hint that he still lived, might sign Nita's death warrant.

His thoughts flashed back to Willis Fleming....

FLEMING WAS no personal friend of Wentworth's. Little more than an acquaintance, he was a society weakling rather than a ne'er-do-well. The foster-son of wealthy old Hulbert Fleming, Willis' sensational escapades had been a constant source of grief to the old man. Somehow, he had managed to last his way through college and medical school and had served his internship in the Fleming Hospital, a private institution which Hulbert Fleming had established and endowed especially for his benefit.

Head of that hospital was Dr. Emil Anderson, a skilled physician whom old Hulbert had engaged to supervise and train Willis—a professional nurse and guardian to watch the madcap and keep him out of trouble.

Willis, Wentworth knew, could have been calling him for no mere social purpose—their relations were not of that sort. He must have been in trouble, grave trouble—known that death hung over him—and been unable to secure help in time to ward it off....

By early afternoon the writer who had linked Wentworth's death with Fleming's had made further progress.

"Another Beckoning Finger Death," he headed his column, beneath it an account of the passing of Moses Altheim, a retired jeweler, who had died in his sleep a week ago. One of the grisly etchings had been found hanging in his bedroom—though intimates testified they had never seen the thing before and had no idea how it came there! Spurred on by this discovery, the writer had burrowed deeper into the obituary column and uncovered nearly a dozen similar deaths—men of wealth who recently had passed away while asleep, apparently without cause other than a stroke or heart failure.

These were no coincidences, Wentworth knew at once. They were linked together, separate parts of a dastardly plot—and because he, himself, had in some way become enmeshed in its web, Nita's life was nearly snuffed out!

Grimly, he re-envisioned that sudden attack on his car, and back into his mind flashed the tense face of Tony Morelli bending over the wheel of the murder car. Tony Morelli....

Out of the filing cabinet of his memory came the Morelli folder.

Tony Morelli was an East Side gangster long immune to arrest because of his political power. His brother, Vic Morelli, less skillful in sidestepping the law, had been convicted of extortion and recently completed a term in Sing Sing prison. While sojourning up the river, Vic had been the central figure in a prison scandal, when it was discovered that he was comfortably ensconced in a soft hospital assignment. Investigators had charged that he possessed no qualifications whatever for the job, and that his brother's political influence had chiseled it for him.

Reviewing the case, Wentworth remembered that "Doc" Roth, a physician who had lost his license and gone to jail for malpractice, had defended Morelli—testifying that he had discovered that Vic possessed a natural aptitude for medicine and was an invaluable hospital aid. Vic Morelli was at present back in circulation, but Doc Roth—Wentworth wondered where the quack doctor might be.

Headquarters would know about Roth, and while headquarters was now closed to Richard Wentworth it was still open to Terry Trimble. Sergeant O'Shaughnessy, of the Detective Bureau, was Trimble's confidant. Wentworth called the bureau, got the sergeant on the phone and disguised his voice to simulate Trimble's soft-slurred half-accent.

"Doc Roth?" O'Shaughnessy echoed his question. "Sure, he's out. The parole board turned him loose. You won't be losin' any money if you risk a bet that Tony Morelli had his fine Eyetalian hand in the deal. Doc had his comin'-out party about two weeks ago, an' the Morellis took him in charge the minute he got back to town."

Doc Roth was back in town with the Morellis... Two weeks—that period would cover all of the dozen sleeping deaths the *Enquirer* writer had listed. And Tony Morelli had been at the wheel of the death-car that swooped down upon Nita and the supposed Wentworth... Who were the other occupants of that car—the ones who actually had hurled the infernal machine—Vic Morelli and Doc Roth? Wentworth had nothing but a nebulous theory on which to base his suspicion. But his strong-fingered hands balled into white-knuckled fists as he considered that possibility. He determined to investigate the activities of the Morellis.

THE EAST Side saloon, of which Tony was part owner, was the most likely place to locate them. But when Wentworth arrived at the dingy place, only half a dozen idlers were at the bar and the back room was empty. Watchfully, he took up his vigil at one end of the bar until he noticed the bartender eyeing him suspiciously.

"I been hoping Tony or Vic would come in," he mumbled to the liquor dispenser the next time that heavy-faced individual came and stood, glowering, in front of him. "Know when they're likely to be around?"

"Dunno—they ain't here," was the growled response. "Ain't seen them t'day." But the fellow's murky eyes narrowed and the hostility on his ugly face became unmistakable.

With clumsy craft, the barkeep sidled to the other end of the bar and mumbled something to a rat-faced individual who perked up his head like a pointing dog. Almost immediately, Rat-face downed his drink and left. When Wentworth followed him, a few minutes later, it took no skill to spot him and a companion eyeing the barroom door from a hallway across the way. He watched them, as they trailed him—and gave them the slip at a convenient cross-street.

The Morellis unquestionably were back home in their old haunts and up to something important—but taking precautions that none but those they knew and trusted should locate them.

In two other likely rendezvous Wentworth made guarded inquiries, but the bleak hostility and contemptuous silence his feelers elicited told him that he would get nowhere in this fashion. For the time being, he admitted regretfully, he was checked. To go any further, in his present guise, would simply be to butt his head against a stone wall—or run into certain violence.

So far, the Morellis had yielded nothing. Now Willis Fleming, and the peculiar circumstances of his death, still remained to be investigated.

Willis had seldom been at home in the Fleming mansion on one of the exclusive side streets just off Fifth Avenue. He had spent most of his time, and had met his death, in a luxurious penthouse he maintained on the roof of a Murray Hill apartment house. His body had been removed to a funeral chapel, and in all probability the penthouse was now untenanted, deserted even by his valet.

Wentworth decided to take a chance on that. The contents of those rooms might throw some light on the cause of Willis' death—if they had not already been cleaned out.

THERE WAS no evidence of police surveillance when Wentworth stepped into the lobby of the building, and nobody attempted to question him when he took the elevator up to within two floors of the top. The rest of the way he went on foot, unhindered as he climbed to the roof and stood outside the dark, silent penthouse.

Warily, he reconnoitered the roof, to make certain no guards were posted here. Then he stepped to one of the casement windows, took out a tiny glass-cutter and went to work. When a small circle of glass dropped out into his hand, he reached inside and turned the metal handle, waited a moment after the window creaked open, then stepped inside—drawing the casement closed after him.

There was no sound in those rooms except the barely audible whisper of his own breath... yet immediately he sensed that he was *not* alone....

19

For what seemed an eternity, he poised there while his eyes strove to acclimate themselves to the darkness; ears strained to pick up the tiniest rustle of sound....

And then he heard it! From one of the rooms came a metallic clink that was quickly muffled.

His eyes now accustomed to the darkness, he could see that he was in a bedroom. Noiselessly, he cat-footed his way to the darker rectangle of a doorway, crouched there, and then stepped into the little hallway beyond. Half a dozen more steps, and he drew himself up silently at the edge of another doorway, peering into the gloom of the apartment's living room.

Again came that metallic click—then the faintest of squeaks, followed almost instantly by an involuntary, half-smothered gasp.

Crouched low, he moved into the room. His eyes were magneted to a spot of light—the narrow beam of a flashlight now low against one wall... a spot of light almost blotted out by two dark figures huddled in front of it. With infinite caution, Wentworth crept forward until he was halfway across the room, sheltered behind a big easy chair.

From this vantage point he could make out the figures—a man and a woman. The man was on his knees in front of the open door of a wall safe. The woman bent over beside him, eagerly running her fingers through the pigeonholes, leafing through sheaves of papers—when suddenly the room was flooded with blinding light.

"Don't move!" an icy voice clipped short the gasp of terrified surprise that escaped from the woman in front of the safe. "Stay just as you are—unless you want to drop where you stand!" The voice of the newcomer—a woman—was hard, brittle, cold.

For a moment, Wentworth stared at the strange tableau in front of him—the ashen-faced girl, her eyes round and wide with fright, still half-bent over the safe, the ugly-faced thug on his knees, only daring to half-glance over his shoulder... and the frozen-faced woman with the gun.

"I expected visitors tonight," her chill voice clipped again. Wentworth sensed that the speaker had not seen him and was aware only of the presence of the other two.

SO SLOWLY that his body hardly seemed to move, Wentworth inched his head forward until he could see around the side of the chair. Tense and watchful, the woman's finger coiled around the trigger of a revolver held steadily on the two in front of her. She stood in the doorway—a dark-haired, cameo-faced young woman whom he recognized as Sylvia Lane, Willis Fleming's former mistress. Now all softness and beauty had gone from her face. Her clear-cut features were twisted into a bleak sneer, dark eyes gleaming with malignant triumph.

"You realize you are house-breakers," she lashed at her helpless captives. "You realize what I can do to you. Who are you? What are you after? Speak up quickly!"

"I don't know nothin' about it," whined the thug, whom Wentworth now recognized as Sam Pavvy, a safecracker he often had seen and rubbed elbows with in underworld resorts. "I just done what she said—" His voice died away, awed.

Sylvia Lane snapped at the white-faced girl, "Who are you—and what did you take out of that safe?"

Wentworth could see that the girl's blue eyes were wide with terror. Her teeth bit into her under-lip, and not a sound came from her.

"You'll talk, don't worry about that," the chilled-steel voice assured her. "You'll talk now or discover how unpleasant it is to have a dum-dum bullet tear through your belly!" The dark eyes became seething pinpoints, the thin lips pressed together in an almost colorless line. Her fingers drew back on the trigger—and in that second Wentworth knew that he was about to witness cold-blooded murder.

Springing from behind the chair, he catapulted himself across the room, batted her arm upward just as the gun roared and sent its leaden slug crashing harmlessly through a windowpane. Like a tigress she whirled on him, lashing at him with the weapon. But Wentworth's fingers closed around her wrist, twisted it backward.

Screaming with pain and rage, she kicked and spat, tore at him blindly with her free hand, until the revolver dropped from her nerveless fingers. Wentworth flung her staggering back against the doorway as he dived and scooped up the weapon for which Sam Pavvy was already hopefully scrambling.

With the revolver muzzle jammed in his face, Pavvy backed away fearfully. He cringed beside the blonde-haired girl, who still stood transfixed, unable to make a move to help herself. Unlike her, Sylvia Lane, once more on her feet, was panting breathlessly, smoldering eyes brimming with rage as she glanced hopefully over Wentworth's shoulder... toward the living-room door.

"You have the upper hand now," she gritted, "but—"

"No, we're not waiting for any of your playmates to come to your rescue," Wentworth anticipated her thought. "You're going into that closet." With the weapon, he forced her back toward a clothes closet in the penthouse foyer. "While you're cooling off in there, the rest of us will go somewhere else for our chat."

At the last moment, she made a desperate grab for the weapon. Before she could seize it, he had yanked the closet door open and thrust her inside. Then he turned the key in the lock, whirled on Pavvy.

"We're going downstairs and out of this building," he instructed evenly, and his tone made the safecracker wilt. "This gun won't be in your ribs, but it will be trained on you every minute of the way. If you think you can make a break—"

"You got me wrong, boss," Pavvy whimpered. "I'm not pullin' no fast ones with a gun at my spine. I'll do like you say."

Seemingly eager to ingratiate himself, he led the way to the elevator, careful to make no slightest move that might be misconstrued. Wordlessly, the girl walked at his side, her cheeks as white as the little bundle of papers still tightly clutched in her hand.

Wentworth warily scanned the lobby, when they stepped out of the car. It seemed to be empty. Alertly, he followed a pace in the rear as Pavvy and the girl stepped out into the street. They obeyed his low-spoken command and started to cross the sidewalk to the curb... when suddenly something leaped on Wentworth's back, spun him halfway around and then smashed at his head, sending him reeling backward groggily.

Out of the shadows close to the wall of the building, a man and a woman had leaped with scarcely a sound. Wentworth saw the man come charging down on him again. Desperately, he tried to drag the gun from his pocket as he strove to keep on his feet. But the weapon caught in the cloth of his coat—and then it was as if an ax-handle crashed down over the top of his head.

Dazed by that stunning blow, Wentworth felt himself reeling, going down. A ham-like hand caught him in mid-air, fastened on his shoulder, bent him over half-backward—held him helpless there while its ponderous mate whipped up and came slashing down like a gun-butt on his skull. Like the waves of a bottomless sea, darkness closed over him and forced him downward... downward into fathomless depths of smothering blackness....

CHAPTER 3
SLEEPING DEATH

WHEN WENTWORTH came back to his senses, he was lying on a wooden bench in the lobby of the apartment house, with the doorman and one of the elevator operators trying to revive him. His head was still ringing from the effect of that clubbing blow, and waves of nausea swept over him as he grasped the sides of the bench and forced himself to sit up.

"They had a car waiting at the corner—the fellow that jumped you and the woman with him," the doorman was saying. "They hopped in it and was off down the street before I could get a look at the number." He went on doubtfully, "The two that was with you—they ran off and left you lying here."

But Wentworth hardly heard him. Through his pounding brain was flashing a kaleidoscopic recollection of that brief struggle on the sidewalk—the blonde girl being pinned against the wall by the attacking woman; her clothes searched quickly and thoroughly while she vainly struggled; her despairing scream just before darkness engulfed him.

That pile-driving blow on his head... He had recognized neither of the attackers, but there had been something familiar about the man! Now he remembered a day at police headquarters when he sat watching the lineup and Kirkpatrick compelled one of the paraded thugs to go through the motions of his specialty. That thug had been called "Hammer"....

Wentworth was still trying to recall the gangster's last name, next morning, when the newspaper headlines proclaimed the latest development in what was now being called the Sleeping Death. Three more prominent citizens had succumbed to this mysterious malady, their lives ended without warning... three men who had gone to sleep, in the best of health, and never again opened their eyes!

In each case, the fatal beckoning-hand etching was present like a talisman of death. It had been framed on the wall in front of the closed eyes of Maurice Siegel, banker; slipped under the locked door of the bedroom in which Harold Munson, cotton-broker, slept his last sleep; in the topmost envelope of the mail that John Whitney, automobile magnate, would never read.

No longer was there any question about the connection between that grisly summons and the death that struck so silently.

Again the feature writer of the *Enquirer* was on hand with a scoop. He had uncovered an unidentified man who admitted that he was an extortion victim.

"I received a demand for money. I'm not saying how much, because I'm taking no chances of having this traced back to me," he was reported as saying. "It was printed beneath one of those etchings—a picture of a skeleton hand held up, palm forward, as if to block the way. Rather than take chances with my life, I paid. I'm thankful now that I did; or I would probably be like those poor fellows who died in their sleep. I paid—but I'm getting out of this city where a man isn't safe in his own bed!"

This one man was known to have paid extortion money, but how many dozens, or hundreds, were keeping discreetly silent? Wentworth began to appreciate the magnitude of the criminal deviltry against which he was fighting—the fiendish scheme gaining momentum like a landslide juggernauting downhill as each additional fatality added to the terror of the Sleeping Death!

Tony Morelli, secure in his underworld hideout, was the closest link to the perpetrator of this reign of terror, but now there were others. Sam Pavvy and the yellow-haired girl; this man Hammer and the vixen who had been with him; the vitriolic-tempered Sylvia Lane. In some way, they all tied up with this thing. But, with the exception of Pavvy, they were as elusive as the Morellis. Pavvy undoubtedly would prove to be the easiest to locate, the most willing to talk once pressure was applied.

WENTWORTH HAD already started for the door when the telephone halted him, drew him back into the apartment. For a moment he hesitated, then lifted the instrument from its cradle.

"Hello, Trimble," a voice rich in its Irish burr came over the wire. "O'Shaughnessy. You were askin' about Doc Roth yesterday. Thought you might be interested to know that one of the boys got a squint at him last night. What makes you interested in that lug, anyway? Got anything on him you wanna come down here and tell us about?"

"No—no police stuff." Wentworth concentrated on imitating Terry Trimble's voice. "One of my clients used to be a patient of the Doc's and thinks he's entitled to a bit of refund. He'd like to meet him again."

"Well, he's in town all right," the sergeant grumbled, "and drawin' crooks to him like a magnet. We picked up half a dozen out-of-town yeggs yesterday—and there's reports of a couple dozen more being seen down in Morelli's district. Better tell your man to watch his step."

Out-of-town crooks flocking to New York, to Morelli's district! Thoughtfully Wentworth lowered the phone as he considered the significance of that bit of information. Undoubtedly, it meant that the Morellis were organizing, recruiting a criminal army—an army of extortion to enforce the demands backed up by some inexplicable death conceived in the devilishly cunning brain of wily Doc Roth?

That seemed to be the explanation. The timing of this terrifying scourge, Tony Morelli being in the murder car the night

RICHARD WENTWORTH

Wentworth's machine was bombed, the inexplicable nature of these sleeping deaths—all jibed with that theory. But where did Sam Pavvy fit into the picture? Was Pavvy working for the Morellis? Was that why he had been there in Willis Fleming's penthouse, robbing Fleming's safe after the Morellis had eliminated Willis with the Sleeping Death?

If that was the answer, Sam Pavvy was the weakest link in the Morellis' chain, for he would talk, lead the way to his masters....

HALF AN hour later, Wentworth rang the bell of the four-story tenement that was Sam Pavvy's residence. Even more tumble-down and unsavory looking than its disreputable neighbors, this ancient rat's-nest rooming-house had its advantages. Chief of these was old Maggie, the keen-eyed hag who finally shuffled to the door—old Maggie, whose widespread acquaintance made her a veritable *Who's Who* of the underworld, and whose instinct for spotting detectives was unerring.

Maggie said she didn't know whether Sam Pavvy was in or not, and didn't seem to care, as she shrugged her bent shoulders and shuffled back into her own smelly quarters. But Wentworth knew that, before he had mounted the first flight of steps, a

buzzer was sounding in Pavvy's top-floor quarters to warn him to be on his guard.

When he reached the upper hallway, he walked to Pavvy's door and stood in front of it as he knocked. No response… except the slight sound that told of furtive movements behind the portal. Stepping to one side of the door, out of range of the peek-hole with which he knew it was equipped, Wentworth waited a few minutes and then knocked again. Then he turned quickly and tiptoed to the farther end of the corridor, where a doorway led to a ladder topped by a roof-scuttle.

Up the ladder and across the catwalk that led to the fire escape—and, in less than a minute after his knock, Wentworth eased himself down onto the first landing. He peered into Sam Pavvy's room over his leveled automatic, as the safecracker still crouched with his ear against his door. A tap on the window brought Pavvy bolt upright, then trembling across the room, wide-eyed with amazement, as Wentworth raised the sash and stepped inside.

"Geez!" Pavvy wondered aloud. "How'n hell didja know where to find me? How didja know—"

"I'm asking the questions, Pavvy," Wentworth cut him short. "And this time you won't have your pals waiting outside the building to jump me when I leave."

"I don't know nothin' about that," the weasel-faced thug protested. "I never seen them before. All I know, we come out o' that joint an' a feller lands on your back. A dame jumps the gal—an' I didn't wait for nothing more. I scrammed."

"What were you doing there in Willis Fleming's apartment?" Wentworth switched his talk. "Why did you open his safe?" His eyes were sharp as he waited.

"I don't know nothin' about that," Pavvy protested again. "Just like I told that gal that stuck us up, I don't know nothin'. All I know is that the gal—the one I was with—paid me to go up there with her an' crack the crib. She said there wouldn't be no trouble."

"Who was that girl you were with?"

"Miss Cahill—she's a nurse in the Fleming Hospital," Pavvy supplied readily. "She took care o' me when I was laid up there after an accident. That was about a year ago. I didn't see nothin' of her till the other day when she come here an' wants me to help her with this job she hadda pull. I don't know nothin' more'n that."

And apparently he didn't. Wentworth prodded him further, but not even the threatening gun muzzle could drag more information out of Pavvy or make him admit any connection with the Morellis.

"Me an' Tony—we don't love each other none." He scowled. "He wouldn't let me in on his racket, even if I wanted any part of it."

But, for the moment, Wentworth had lost interest in the Morellis. The blonde who had paid to have Willis Fleming's safe opened was a nurse in the Fleming Hospital! That was far more significant. The trail was getting warmer, and he was eager to follow it—to get up to the hospital and see whether Nurse Cahill was still there.

SHE WAS not in. He learned that as soon as he had paid off

31

his taxi and stepped into the ether-odored reception room of the Upper West Side brownstone mansion that Hulbert Fleming had converted into a hospital. She had left in response to a phone call less than half an hour before. Wentworth cursed himself for not bringing Sam Pavvy along with him, or at least leaving the safecracker tied up and gagged.

Doretta Cahill was not in, but Dr. Emil Anderson was—and he would see Mr. Trimble.

Wentworth found the physician sitting at his desk, a white-uniformed man of medium build, with sharp-featured, ascetic face and high forehead that made him appear balder than he actually was. His dark eyes were bright and birdlike and darted nervous glances about the room as he talked. He rubbed the palms of his hands together agitatedly, tapping one foot on the floor.

The man was obviously worried and more than a little annoyed.

"The unwelcome notoriety which we have received since that ridiculous account of Willis Fleming's death is bad enough, Mr. Trimble," he chattered. "But since then it seems to be just one thing after the other. A hospital must operate on schedule; we can't afford to have our routine interrupted in this way. Not only are we shorthanded by the unfortunate loss of Doctor Fleming, but this morning my pathologist and one of my interns failed to report for duty. And then Miss Cahill received a telephone call and insisted that she be allowed to go off duty immediately—"

"It is Miss Cahill about whom I wanted to see you," Wentworth managed to interrupt. "Perhaps you can tell me something about her private life. I know this may seem irregular, but if you can assist me I may be able to spare you further undesirable publicity in connection with Willis Fleming's death. Can you tell me now, for example, whether young Fleming was interested in her?"

"Really, I know nothing of her personal affairs." Anderson shook his head vigorously. "What the members of my staff do outside the hospital does not concern me—unless, as today, it interferes with their duties. I'm afraid I can't help."

Uncomfortably, he squirmed in his chair, his darting eyes seemingly vainly seeking a way out of the office. Wentworth watched particularly those constantly working hands, noting the scar that disfigured the back of the right, evidently the result of an acid burn.

"The pathologist and this intern you mention—who are they?" he shifted his questioning. "Have you tried to get in touch with them by telephone?"

"Doctor George Holden is our pathologist." The hospital head reached for a desk directory. "He shares an apartment with Eugene Fajans, one of our interns." He read aloud a street address less than a mile from the hospital. "We have tried to reach them, but their telephone doesn't answer. Evidently, they are not at home—which is strange, because Doctor Holden has always been entirely dependable."

That *was* strange, but no stranger than the sudden unexplained departure of Nurse Doretta Cahill, Wentworth considered, as he hailed a taxi and gave the driver the address of Holden's apartment. Perhaps the pathologist would prove to be no lead, but it was possible that he might be able to furnish some clue to the Cahill girl's whereabouts or throw some light on her relations with Willis Fleming.

WENTWORTH LOCATED the apartment without difficulty, but when he pressed the buzzer there was no response. Hesitantly, he turned, on the point of leaving. Then he was almost certain that he had heard, or at least *sensed,* a sound that echoed that buzz. He stood with his ear close to the door, and all was quiet beyond it. On a hunch, he dropped to his knees and put his head to the floor. Now that he could see through the narrow crack above the threshold, his every nerve tingled!

Somebody was in that apartment; he caught a flicker of shadow on the floor. Again he raised his finger to the buzzer and pressed—and the shadow almost blotted out his view.

Quietly, Wentworth rose and took a clip of skeleton keys from his pocket. Noiselessly, he slipped one into the lock, another. The last one did the trick. The bolt clicked back—but when he put his weight against the door, it yielded only a fraction of an inch and then was pushed shut again by someone on the other side.

With his shoulder against the door, at the knob, and his feet braced on the carpeted corridor, Wentworth put all his strength into a heave. The door yielded, opened nearly a foot—sufficient for him to wedge a shoe in the opening and get a fresh grip. From inside the foyer came a gasp, a muffled sob—and then the door was pushing open inexorably, for Doretta Cahill's strength was no match for his own!

Wentworth cast one glance at the panting, frightened girl, as he darted past her and ran into the living room. The moment the door opened he felt a draft. Now he understood those sounds he had heard as he forced an entrance. One of the living-room windows was wide open. Someone had just left—fleeing down the fire escape. But when Wentworth reached the window there was no sign of the fugitive.

Quickly, Wentworth turned to halt the girl. But she had made no attempt to leave. She still stood in the foyer, regarding him with wide, horror-filled eyes. Puzzled, he glanced around the living room. An open door, at one side, evidently led into a bedroom. Stepping to the doorway, he glanced inside… and his nerves tensed.

Lying in bed, apparently asleep, was a young man—but it took only a glance at his white face, sagging jaw, to know that from this sleep there would be no awakening!

Wentworth stepped to the bedside. The gray-white cheek was cold, stiff with *rigor mortis.*

There was a rush of footsteps behind him, a gasp—and Doretta Cahill stood staring down at the corpse.

"He didn't do it!" she gasped hysterically. "George didn't do it! He was asleep in his own bedroom—and found the dead man this way! I know you're from the police—you're trying to trap him! But George was his best friend—he wouldn't have harmed him!"

George—that meant George Holden, the pathologist. This latest victim of the Sleeping Death was Eugene Fajans, the intern.

"If George didn't do it, why did he run away?" Wentworth demanded.

"Because…" Like a trapped animal desperately seeking a means of escape, she glanced wildly around the room. Suddenly her eyes widened with new terror. "Oh, my God!" burst from her blood-drained lips, before she could clamp them shut.

Tight-lipped, she faced him from where she had backed in front of Fajans' dresser.

Wentworth saw that she was trying to conceal something. She was holding something behind her back, edging toward the door. Quickly, he intercepted her. Despite her struggles, he imprisoned her hands—and forced from her clutch a framed etching of Death's beckoning finger!

Wentworth realized that the man who had just left the apartment was George Holden. But what had the pathologist had to do with this death? How much did he know about it? Why had he been attempting to conceal it instead of reporting to the police?

He tried, once more, to question the girl—but she was beyond answering, sobbing hysterically.

Irresolutely, he paced the apartment, then stopped as he passed the telephone. That phone had not answered when Dr. Anderson tried to call Holden or Fajans. The hospital number was printed on a little card hanging from the mouthpiece, and Wentworth dialed it to report developments to the superintendent. But the line was busy.

He tried again. Rapidly, he told Anderson what had transpired.

"Fajans dead!" the physician's startled exclamation came. Wentworth could hear him catch his breath. "Good God, what next? Mr. Fleming just called me. I was sitting here trying to make out what he had said, when you rang. He was so excited I could hardly understand him. It was something about being afraid—terribly afraid...."

Hulbert Fleming, afraid—so terrified that he was calling for aid... Just as his foster-son, Willis, had tried to call!

WENTWORTH SLAMMED the receiver onto its hook and streaked out of that apartment. Catching a taxi on the run, he leaped inside and shouted the address of the Fleming mansion, which was almost directly across Central Park from the hospital.

The mansion stood on a corner, and, as he sprang from the cab and raced up the short flight of stone steps in front of the entrance, he saw a man dart out of a side door. For a split-second, the fellow turned, and Wentworth would have sworn that it was the face of Dr. Anderson....

But that was impossible—at that moment, Anderson was on the other side of town! Even had he left the hospital right after Wentworth, he could not possibly have negotiated the distance in time to reach the mansion before Wentworth arrived!

He shrugged the idea off, as he sped up the steps, reached the wide door. It yielded to his grip, and he stepped into the broad hall—and such utter silence that made him fear he was too late. Quickly, he went from room to room, calling the old man's name. Nowhere was there a sign of life until he opened the door of

Hulbert Fleming's bedroom… and then what confronted did not look like life but death.

The room was rapidly filling with a choking gas. It seemed to generate from a pail beside the ornate four-poster bed in which lay the old aristocrat, his eyes closed as if in sleep—or death!

Clasping one hand over his nostrils, Wentworth reached the nearest window, unlocked it, flung it wide open. Without waiting to take a breath, he spun on his heel and ran back for that pail of hell's brew, dumped its contents out into the yard—then hung out over the windowsill while he filled his lungs with fresh air.

As soon as he dared, he strode to the bed and lifted Fleming. For a moment, as he bent over the old man, his eyes glimpsed the framed picture hanging in front of the bed—grisly Death beckoning to him. Then he had the unconscious man in his arms, dragging him out of the room—cheating the Grim Reaper of his prey!

In the untainted air of the hallway Hulbert Fleming gasped for breath, and his eyes soon blinked open. Uncomprehendingly, he looked around—then shrank from something, or someone, he thought he saw in front of him. His lips moved weakly, and Wentworth bent close to catch the faint words.

"Jes-sie…" The whispered syllables were hardly intelligible. "Don't, Jes-sie. It… wasn't… my fault. No… no!" His voice was becoming stronger, rising in fear. "You *can't* do that to me!"

And then he realized where he was, what he was saying—and instantly shut his lips.

"What happened?" Wentworth pressed. "Who is Jessie?

What did she do to you? You've almost been murdered, man. Unless you speak up, whoever tried to kill you will escape."

But now Fleming was in full control of his senses. His jaw set firmly, and, as Wentworth stared into the thin, patrician-featured face, he saw that it would be useless to question further—Fleming would tell him nothing. That death etching might scare him into an admission....

Getting it from the bedroom wall, Wentworth suddenly confronted him with the thing, demanding to know how it had come there.

Curiously, the old man examined it. "I never saw this one before," he said matter-of-factly. "There was another—a print of a skeleton hand that came with a demand for money. I ignored that, and this probably is the result. Now that I know what to expect, I shall take proper precautions in the future."

And with that unperturbed admission Wentworth had to be satisfied.

CHAPTER 4
MURDERING MORPHEUS

WITH IMPUNITY, the Sleeping Death struck down its victims—leaving, in its trail, only mystification or baffling silence. It had cut down Willis Fleming, and its rapier thrust had licked out greedily for his foster-father. Young Eugene Fajans had been stricken in his bed. Yet, of those who might have been able to throw some light on his fate, Dr. Emil Anderson professed complete ignorance, George Holden and

Doretta Cahill had disappeared, and Hulbert Fleming would say nothing. Sam Pavvy vehemently protested his innocence, Sylvia Lane could not be located, and Wentworth did not even know the identity of his assailant, Hammer, or the woman who had been with him.

Of all the leads Wentworth had encountered, Tony Morelli seemed to offer the most. Tony Morelli, he resolved, would solve the riddle. Once he located Tony Morelli, there would be ques-

He dragged him across the stricken bar room—
that much he owed the man for past favors.

tions for the gangster-politician to answer—a score to settle that was mounting higher each day that Nita van Sloan lay suffering as the result of that murderous attack!

Terry Trimble could get nowhere in such a quest; he was as helpless to penetrate Tony Morelli's underworld hideouts as Richard Wentworth would have been. Those resorts were open only to the initiate, accredited members of the criminal fraternity… and so it was as one of them Wentworth now became.

Deep in the slums this other character lived and had his being—resident of an evil-smelling tenement on a noisome, squalid canyon of a street lost in that rabbit warren of impoverished humanity which lies east of the Bowery. His fellow denizens of Holian Alley called this man Blinky McQuade and knew him only as a hermit-like safecracker who came and went among them, disappearing for weeks at a time as the exigencies of his profession required.

At first regarded only as a has-been hanger-on of the fringes of the underworld, Blinky had gradually established his reputation and gained their confidence so that the most exclusive criminal rendezvous were now open to him—which was exactly what Richard Wentworth had planned when he conceived and gave Blinky McQuade to the world….

Dismissing the cab that had brought him downtown from Hulbert Fleming's mansion, Wentworth got out several blocks from his destination and journeyed the rest of the way afoot. Unobtrusively, he mingled with the shabby, shifty-eyed men, dirty-faced children, raucous-voiced women, haggling with hole-in-the-wall merchants, until he reached the end of Holian Alley, where it formed a sharp V with equally dingy Pallin Place.

The drab, four-story tenement that was Number One Holian Alley was where he was headed—an ideal location for Blinky McQuade and his neighbors because the triangular little court that was the back yard for Number One, and the corresponding building on Pallin Place, afforded an entrance and exit through both buildings—a circumstance that, on more than one occasion, had proved invaluable to him.

Stepping through the dirty, paint-peeled vestibule, Wentworth went up the creaking stairs to a rear room on the second floor. Inside, he drew the grimy shades and turned to the mammoth-size bed that was the principal article of furniture in the shabby, plaster-cracked cubbyhole. Kneeling in the center, he pressed his fingers against secret springs concealed in the massive headboard. They released a panel which opened out to become a perfectly equipped makeup shelf in front of a brightly lighted mirror.

Expertly, he went to work. In an incredibly short time, the features of Terry Trimble faded, merged into those of Richard Wentworth, and then were transformed into the frowsy, pendulous-lipped countenance of the shambling safecracker whose eyes, injured by a premature blast of "soup," had to be protected by a pair of thick-lensed, metal-hooded spectacles. Wash and powder turn his black hair from a carrot-red to a dirty gray; then came an outfit of ragged and none too clean clothes… and Blinky McQuade shuffled to the door, secure in the knowledge that not even the closest friends of Richard Wentworth would

have given this seedy-looking nonde-
script a second glance.

From Holian Alley, Blinky now made
his way from one familiar resort to the
other. Saloons, clubs, poolrooms, stores
that were only blinds for the bookmak-
er's headquarters in the rear, "hotels"
whose guests were interested only in the
narcotics that went with the beds they
hired—places where he rubbed elbows with thieves and killers,
underworld scum wanted in half the states of the Union. A nod
and a mumbled "h'ya" were his open sesame. Without question,
they accepted him. But the moment he started making inquiries about the Morellis, he noticed a change in the atmosphere.

Eyes that had merely glanced in his direction now bored into
him suspiciously. Men with whom he had been talking froze up
and lost interest. Decidedly, something was afoot—but Blinky
McQuade seemed no closer to discovering its nature than Terry
Trimble had been—

Not until he passed the eagle-eyed guard at the door and
shuffled up to the bar of Balmy's Bit House.

IN THAT gathering place of the elite of crimedom, where
none but the graduates of the nation's penitentiaries were
permitted to enter, he was quick to notice something unusual
in the air. Balmy's had become a house divided, his customers
separated into two camps. The larger of the two groups regarded
the other with open hostility and contempt. Those, in turn, stood

back with the attitude of men confidently waiting for the vindication they knew would come.

Deaf to the slurring remarks aimed at them, oblivious to the contemptuous glances, they grinned and waited….

The smaller fry, these, Blinky noticed. The bigger men, ex-convicts accustomed to lead their fellows, ignored them and stood around the bar or gathered in the booths to grumble their displeasure. Gradually, as his listening ears caught fragments of their conversation, Blinky began to understand the situation.

These big shots of crime were wrought up over someone who was attempting to ride roughshod over them—were in open rebellion at what they considered an attempt to dragoon them.

Sourest of all was Balmy himself. " 'Lo, Blinky," he grunted as he sidled up beside McQuade and poured himself a glass of whisky. "Ain't seen you for weeks. What you been doin'—out organizin' for the union?"

"Whatcha mean—*union?*" Blinky looked over the top of his glass, studied Balmy's broken-nosed, ring-scarred face. "Kiddin' me?"

"Union of all the pickpockets an' penny-snatchers," the ex-pugilist snarled sufficiently loudly so that his voice carried the full length of the bar. "All the panhandlers are signin' up an' takin' their orders from the new big boss. But when he thinks he can send orders around here, an' try to tell me how to run my place, he's got another guess comin'!"

Growls of approval echoed from all corners of the place, and a burly six-footer, who proudly boasted that his was the oldest name on the G-men's list of public enemies, pushed his way forward.

"He's found out that he can't run this town the way he pleases," he snorted. "Now he's bringing in a lot of foreign rods to help him run his bluff. But we'll take care of all those rats from Chi and Detroit, the rest of the hick towns. Let 'em come—"

He coughed and tried to clear his throat… and suddenly the coughing and throat-clearing had become an epidemic.

"Hell, where's that damn bartender?" Balmy roared as he reached over the bar and tried to pour himself a chaser. "Where the—"

The bartender had disappeared from his post, Blinky noticed—and in the same instant noticed several other things. The air in the crowded room was more stuffy than usual. He could hardly breathe; many of the others were leaning heavily against the bar, nodding over the tables. The members of that smaller, despised group had all disappeared, only Balmy's cronies and sympathizers remaining….

Suddenly suspicious, Blinky hurried to the door and tried to open it. It would not budge. He pounded on it, but there was no response from the sentinel who should have been on guard in the little watch-room beyond. The air was rapidly becoming worse. Nostrils and mouth felt dry, and his throat was like sand-paper. For an instant, he reeled unsteadily, as if with an attack of vertigo. Wild panic rioted in his brain….

He groped groggily back to the bar, past men who were dropping to the floor, falling asleep all around him. Not until then did he notice that one of those grisly etchings of death hung over the center of the back-bar, beckoning Balmy and his customers to the grave! That was it—the place was a death-trap in which they were penned up helplessly!

Blinky clung to the bar for support, searching frantically. The windows—but no use trying to break those bulletproof panes or open them without knowing where the locking mechanisms was located. There was no way out of this death-trap! No way—except one!

HOLDING HIS breath as best he could, his aching lungs bursting, he crouched low and put every ounce of his failing strength into a desperate charge. It carried him across the room headlong against a section of the wall that he knew was only a plaster-board partition. For a moment, it seemed this would hold, that he would be flung back into the room to drop off to sleep and die. Then it gave way before him, crumbling, showering dust into his face as he tumbled through and sprawled on the floor of the storeroom beyond.

Precious seconds he rested on hands and knees, filling his lungs with the untainted air. Then he dashed back into the stricken barroom, found Balmy, grabbed him by the collar and dragged him into the storeroom. Even here relief was only momentary; already the lethal air billowed in through the shattered wall. Only one exit left from this storeroom—a door leading into a corridor that led to the barroom, in one direction, and a dead-end in the other. Only one exit... except the ventilator opening near the ceiling.

Desperately, Blinky piled case on case until he could climb up to the opening and rip the flimsy grating out of its frame. As he suspected, the ventilator opened onto an airshaft. At least, it would be better for Balmy than leaving him lying in the death-filled storeroom.

Every ounce of his strength was needed to lift the heavy Bit House proprietor to his shoulders, stagger with him up the rickety pile of cases—but at last he shoved Balmy through the ventilator aperture, balanced him there a moment, and then dropped him to the bottom of the shaft. That much he owed the man for past favors.

Squeezing through the ventilator himself, he found a hand-hold in the airshaft... another, another. Slowly, precariously, he worked his way upward, until at last he reached the roof-light, jabbed his fist through and finally managed to pry it loose. After that, it was a simple matter to cross to the next roof, climb down the fire escape to the back yard, and then through the cellar to the street.

A simple matter—but all the way Blinky still could feel the chilling breath of Death on the back of his neck. It had been a close call—how terribly close he fully realized when, out in the street, he crossed to the other side and looked up at the blank second-story windows of the Bit House. Not a sign of movement there; not a sound. The quietness of death hung over the place that, in a few short minutes, had become a tomb for nearly fifty men!

Balmy and his customers had dared to defy the rising under-world power—and the Sleeping Death had been their reward. Swift, ruthless punishment, its tale would speed from mouth to mouth with the swiftness of a prairie fire—ominous warning to others who might contemplate disobedience.

As he shuffled back to Holian Alley, Wentworth envisioned an underworld docile and welded into an obedient machine, slaves beneath the constant fear of inevitable death—a frightful weapon in the hands of the unscrupulous devil now forging it. Once more, he vowed grimly that the diabolical scheme would be smashed, its perpetrator unmasked and crushed, if it was the last service the Spider ever rendered to society....

ALWAYS ALERT when he approached his Holian Alley hideout, tonight Wentworth was doubly cautious. Some sixth sense, or perhaps it was his near escape from death, warned him to be careful.

From behind a rattletrap car, parked at the corner, he surveyed the entrance of Number One, the house next door, buildings across the narrow street—and gave fervent thanks for his caution! There, huddled in the doorway opposite his own tenement, was a figure he recognized immediately—Jackson, his chauffeur!

Jackson's gaze was riveted on the entrance of Number One.

Backing away from the car, Wentworth quickly circled the block and came down Pallin Place, until he could observe the doorways of the houses opposite Number Two, the building customarily used for his emergency exit. At first, nobody seemed watching. Then he glimpsed a shifting shadow in one of the areaways. His sharp eyes identified that shadow as old Jenkyns, his butler!

Wentworth understood what their vigil implied. His servants

were suspicious, unconvinced of his death. Jackson knew of his Blinky McQuade personality and had therefore instituted this watch to discover if this explained Wentworth's disappearance. But they *must* believe that he was dead; he must give them no slightest ground for thinking otherwise. Nita's safety demanded it.

If they discovered that he still lived, well-intentioned as they were, they might make some little slip that would once more set the wolves on Nita's trail. Wentworth had kept constantly in touch with Dr. Rogers and knew that, although she was recovering, her condition still was precarious. He must add nothing to her danger, regardless of what it cost to shield her.

This meant that Blinky McQuade, with his invaluable entrées, must also go into retirement with Richard Wentworth. While those faithful watchers were posted at his door, he would not even be able to reach his tenement room for a change of clothing....

Thoughtfully he shuffled back along Pallin Place and remade his plans. First of all, he would have to go to the little garage near the East River. Here a change of clothing and necessary supplies were hidden away in an emergency car kept stored there for just such occasions as this. After he had changed....

BUSILY RESHAPING his plans, he was halfway to the garage when the wail of police sirens brought him up short. Racing wildly, a radio cruiser sped down the almost deserted street and flashed past him. In the distance, others mingled their echoing wails, and then, as he approached the corner, a loaded squad car added to the clamor.

Wentworth caught a glimpse of the reserve squad clinging to their seats, as the patrol careened past. Abruptly, the wail of its siren changed to a shriek of almost human alarm. Startled by that nerve-shattering blast, Wentworth glanced down the semi-dark street. A huge motor delivery truck had backed into it from the cross-street. Instead of keeping to the right, it was in the center of the street, almost completely blocking the narrow way.

The scream of the squad car's brakes added to the shriek of its siren. But instead of attempting to draw to one side, the elephantine truck had come to a halt. Hardly believing his amazed eyes, Wentworth saw that the whole rear of the truck had opened up, dropping outward to form a runway into its dark interior. It happened as quickly as that.

The sides of that truck's stygian maw bristled with men—men with submachine guns held at the ready. This much he saw in the brief flare of a shot—then the squad car was rolling up the ramp, *and the rear of the truck had closed up behind it!*

The thing he had witnessed was fantastic, impossible. Wentworth almost rubbed his eyes to make certain he was not dreaming. A car full of policemen swallowed up by a gargantuan truck in the middle of New York's congested East Side! But he had not been alone in witnessing this incredible performance. Others, like him, had mouths agape, staring at the back of the truck, as if they momentarily expected it to perform even greater wonders.

Nor were they disappointed.

Just as Wentworth started forward to investigate, the rear wall, like a released drawbridge, began to lower again. Out of the dark interior backed the squad car. On the pavement again, its gears shifted. It started forward, climbed the curbstone to pass the blockading truck, and proceeded on its way as if not a thing in the world had interrupted its course. Apparently, it was just as it had been before the truck swallowed it—but Wentworth's sharp eyes had noticed one marked change. The patrolmen were buttoning their coats and adjusting their hats now when the insensate monster again spewed them forth....

Breathlessly, Wentworth raced after it, trailing the wailing siren for several blocks. By the time he caught up with it, the car was the center of an excited throng. The officers had gotten out and were trying to restore order in front of a large tenement house. They had formed a cordon to prevent anyone approaching too near its closed doorway.

Something was going on inside that building—nobody in the milling crowd seemed to know just what. The windows were closed, and not a sound came from its eight stories. Yet an indefinable air of ghastly tragedy hung over the place. Wentworth felt a prickling of his skin....

Working his way through the rapidly swelling throng, he paused at its edge beside a radio car drawn up at the curb. Something about that car had caught his eye. A splash of blood had trickled down the door beside the steering wheel. When he tested it with his finger, it proved fresh blood, still wet and sticky.

Curiously, he poked his head through the open window. Something was huddled on the car floor—the battered-headed corpse of a policeman left there, unheeded, by his fellows!

Farther down the block Wentworth found another radio car, another corpse! Slumped flat in the seat behind the wheel, head bashed in by a terrific blow, was the body of the driver! The third uniformed corpse Wentworth found wedged behind two ash cans, a telltale foot protruding just far enough to betray its hiding place. Three murdered policemen… and God, alone, knew how many more were being trodden underfoot by that unheeding crowd!

Three murdered policemen—and suddenly Wentworth knew how they had died. Shouldering through the gaping throng, he worked his way up to the uniformed cordon, got a look at the faces of several of those bluecoats. And now he understood the whole set-up—what had really occurred during that fantastic car-swallowing performance!

Retreating through the crowd, he dived into the nearest cellar-way—gripped by mingled horror and rage. Wholesale murder was being perpetrated in this slum street—unchecked because those who should have prevented it, the paid guardians of law and order, had been the first to die! The police were worse than helpless—*they were dead!*

He, alone, could hope to stop these murdering devils.

Swiftly, Wentworth's expert fingers went to work with the makeup kit that now came from inside the lining of his coat. Crouched in the darkness, between piles of rubbish, with only the tiny ray of a pocket-flash playing on his face, he tore down the frowsy countenance of Blinky McQuade. He transformed it into a thing of nightmare horror—a hideous, leering mask that had stricken abject terror into the heart of many a criminal monster who had proudly boasted that he knew no fear.

Back at Wentworth, from the little metal mirror, stared an

incredibly ugly face with shaggy eyebrows and snaggly teeth set in a slit of a mouth repulsively lipless. A demoniacal face was framed with lanky strands of matted black hair, as a close-fitting wig went into place, and then was topped with a floppy-brimmed black felt hat that came out of the lining of Wentworth's vest. A long, sweeping black cape whipped out from beneath his shirt—and the Spider was ready!

CREEPING OUT from the black hole that had just spawned him, the Spider scurried across the sidewalk to one of the radio cars, clambered onto its roof, and filled the night with an eerie howl—a fiendish, half-maniacal cackle that riveted every eye on him and chilled the blood in the veins of the petrified watchers!

Before the amazed cordon of bluecoats could raise a hand against that crouching monstrosity, the Spider's twin automatics were blazing like machine guns, decimating their ranks with deadly accurate lead. Like a great bat, the black cape flapping around his ears, he leaped from his perch, straight into the panic-stricken crowd that melted away before him as if he were the Angel of Death. A scattered fusillade of shots greeted him as he charged the cordon, but few of those uniformed targets had the stomach to stand against his guns—and when someone loudly bellowed, "The Spider!" their rout was complete. Pell-mell into the crowd they thrust themselves, seeking shelter behind human shields.

Unhindered, the Spider raced across the sidewalk to the tenement door, yanked it open and leaped into the dimly-lit vestibule. For a moment he stood silhouetted there in the doorway, while his deadly guns brought down two of the hardier killers, who had thought to shoot him in the back. Then the door slammed behind him—and a bullet splintered one of its panels, a promise and warning of what awaited any who dared follow.

The moment he was past the inner door, Wentworth stopped to get his bearings. As he expected, the usually bedlam-like tenement was as quiet as the tomb—which he now feared it was!

Racing up the uncarpeted stairs to the floor above, he ran to the front of the building and tried two of the apartment doors. Both were locked, but when he rattled them with his fist he knew that they would not stand up under an assault. Drawing back a few yards, he hurled himself forward, heard the panels splintering as the flimsy lock snapped—then pitched into the cheaply-furnished room—*of death!*

Tied to chairs in that humble kitchen were an old woman and her two daughters, heads drooping to one side, eyes closed. Asleep? Asleep never to awaken! The throat-constricting air in that room told him how they had died, even before he saw the beckoning-hand etching pinned on the fly-specked wall....

All this Wentworth saw in a split-second. Then he was across the room, smashing out a windowpane with his automatic. Framed by the broken glass, he leaned out and yelled to the frightened crowd, who backed away the moment his gargoylish face appeared.

"The Spider is your friend!" he reassured them. "It's those fellows in uniform who are your enemies. They are no cops— they're murderers in stolen uniforms. Murderers who have condemned all the tenements of this house to the Sleeping

Death! That's why they kept you out of here—so you would not reach your friends until too late!"

Shots were beginning to bark at him, lead slapping against the building, thudding into the window frame—but he saw that the crowd was wavering, undecided.

Darting back into the room, he lifted one of the bound corpses, held her up in the window, chair and all.

"That's what they've done—in every apartment in this building!" he shouted. The roar of the crowd drowned out his words, as it surged forward, storming through the doorway.

Wentworth met the volunteers, as they came up the stairs, organized and detailed them, warning them lest they fall victims of the strange death that still filled the apartments. Soon the halls reverberated with the sound of splintering wood, crashing doors, shattering windows, as the rescue squads roamed from floor to floor. But most of their work was in vain. Help had been delayed too long, and, before they could be reached, three-quarters of the tenants of that doomed building were dead—ruthlessly slaughtered like trapped rats to demonstrate terrifyingly the unbridled power of this new master of evil who demanded obedience or death!

CHAPTER 5
DEATH INSURANCE

H IS ATTEMPTED salvage in that house of death completed, the Spider darted, unobserved, into one of the stricken apartments—and a few minutes later it was Blinky

McQuade who mingled with the awe-stricken curiosity-seekers now roaming through the halls. By this time fresh squads of police had arrived and were taking charge, emptying the building of all but its eternal sleepers.

Blinky shuffled out to where an excited crowd was gathered around an old, gray-bearded man who shook with terror.

"I didn't know!" he wailed, lifting hands to heaven. *"Mein Gott*—how should I think they would do anything like this? They sent me a letter, yes. They wanted me to pay money, or something should happen to my building. But I have insurance for that. How should I know they would murder my tenants? *Mein Gott*—that something like this should happen!"

With horror-filled eyes the old landlord gazed at the ambulances and undertakers' cars now beginning to arrive. He hardly heard the maledictions the neighbors of the victims were heaping on his head. A broken man, he would be pilloried for not having paid the tribute to prevent this calamity. To punish him for disobeying, more than a hundred lives had been heartlessly sacrificed. To punish him—and to warn other landlords who might be reluctant to comply with extortion demands!

Seething with rage, Wentworth shuffled his way through the crowd and continued his interrupted trip to the little sheet-iron garage where his emergency car was stored. Here he quickly changed clothes, altered his makeup, strode back onto the street as Terry Trimble and soon hailed a cab which took him uptown to Trimble's apartment.

But long after he went to bed he lay tossing sleeplessly while columns of dead faces paraded through his mind's eye. Day by day, the death list was growing… and the Spider swore a grim vengeance!

How appalling that death-list had become Wentworth realized the next morning when he read the newspaper accounts of the night's horrors. The gruesome story of the outrage was featured on the front pages—but it had to share the double-width columns with the accounts of two similar catastrophes in other parts of the city.

Three apartment houses full of people ravaged with death because their owners had refused to pay tribute! Even more terrifying was the dismaying admission that the city's best doctors were helpless, unable to determine the cause of these inexplicable deaths!

In the East Side tenement house, the victims had been knocked out or tied in their chairs by thugs, then left in their locked apartments to die as the Sleeping Death crept over them. But in one of the uptown apartment houses, where death had wiped out nearly every tenant, there had been no sign of an intruder and no attempt at violence.

"Undoubtedly these fatalities are the result of a particularly lethal gas which we have not yet been able to identify," the health commissioner announced. But Wentworth had been in those tenement rooms and the Bit House, when death was raging, and had smelled no gas. He had been conscious of nothing more than an odorless stuffiness, a heaviness in the air that made breathing almost impossible….

Turning away from the grisly accounts which monopolized the news pages, Wentworth glanced through the rest of the paper. His eyes chanced, for a moment, on a Broadway gossip column. Even though Death was stalking unchecked through the metropolis, life in the "hot spots" went on as usual, he observed cynically. Even though men and women were being murdered in their beds, this columnist still found it sufficiently important to chronicle that "Claudette Marvin and Jack Downing are that way about each other"; that "Don Galante and his swing band will go into the 33 Club tomorrow night"; that "some of these lads who try to get too frisky at the Yankee Music Hall forget that Bill Gunther's nickname used to be Hammer—and not because he ever was a shipping clerk."

Hammer! Hammer Gunther! That was the name Wentworth had been trying to dig out of his memory!

Instantly, it was clear to him. Bill Gunther, half-owner of the Yankee Music Hall, a combination theater and dance hall which had been having quite a vogue with its revivals of old melodramas, was Hammer Gunther, the criminal he had seen in the headquarters lineup. Bill Gunther was Hammer Gunther—and only Hammer Gunther could have used his fists in that peculiar head-bashing fashion Wentworth had experienced two nights before.

Bill Gunther was the man who had knocked him out!

Decidedly, Wentworth wanted to know more about Bill Gunther, and the "Ask Us Bureau" of the *Enquirer* seemed the quickest source of information. He dialed the number, and in a few minutes had his answer.

"Bill Gunther has been in show business about two years," the attendant reported. "He started with the Top-Notch, a

59

burlesque theater, sold out his interest in that a year ago and went into partnership with Jessie Ogilvie to open the Yankee Music Hall. Miss Ogilvie is a former actress. She has charge of the production."

There was more, but Wentworth had all that he wanted to

know. Two years—that checked. It was about three years ago that he had seen Gunther in the lineup, and, as he recalled it, the man was discharged at that time for lack of evidence. And his partner was Jessie Ogilvie—

Jessie Ogilvie—Jessie….

That was the name Hulbert Fleming had mentioned as he came to his senses after the attack by the Sleeping Death. He had been muttering about Jessie—a Jessie who had threatened to do something to him. Could this be the same woman?

Wentworth determined to investigate that angle further, but

now there was something more immediate to occupy his attention. He had to attend his own funeral!

From Dr. Rogers, who was keeping in touch with Sutton Place, he had learned that Richard Wentworth was to be buried that morning—and he was particularly interested in watching the ceremony. In all likelihood, he admitted, the burial would be completed without incident. But it was just possible that Tony Morelli, or some of his hoods, might look in to be sure that there actually was a burial....

EVEN BEFORE the funeral party arrived, Wentworth was on hand. He had combed that section of the cemetery to make certain there were no concealed watchers, and then had taken his own position as a supposed visitor to a grave a short distance from his own family plot. From that vantage point, he watched the procession arrive, saw the casket taken from the hearse and carried to the open grave by the sober-faced pallbearers, the mourners filing after it.

Jackson, who had served with him in the trenches of France, was now more grim-faced than Wentworth had seen him during the hottest world war fighting. Ram Singh, dignified son of a noble Sikh family, warrior to his fingertips—even his full beard could not conceal the tight set of his jaw as he followed what he thought were the remains of the man he had fairly adored. Old Jenkyns looked even older in the grief he made no effort to conceal.

It wrenched Wentworth's heart to see their misery—and yet to be able to do nothing about it. He turned his gaze to Stanley Kirkpatrick and the dozen other loyal friends.

Softly over the silent group came the low-spoken words of the commitment. The mourners stepped back, the lowering mechanism began to operate—then the reverent silence was shattered by the roaring clatter of a submachine gun. A  hail of bullets ripped and smashed their way into the descending coffin, sieving it from end to end!

That deadly hail, Wentworth saw at once, came from one of the rear windows of what appeared to be a funeral limousine drawn up at one side of the plot. Instantly, he started toward it, crouching low behind the screening protection of marble monuments which studded the intervening plots. But, swift as he was, Jackson and Ram Singh were faster.

With a speed that told him they had been on the alert for something of this sort, the moment that tommy gun opened up, their weapons were in their hands—blasting lead. Jackson, in the lead, vaulted graves and railings as if back in No Man's Land. The sheer fury of his charge carried him to the limousine before he could be shot down or the startled driver send the machine into motion.

Springing onto the running board, Jackson smashed the middle window with his automatic muzzle. He drew the weapon back for another blow as he tried to yank the door open and get at the machine-gunner. But at that moment the front window shot down. A thug who rode beside the driver reached out and grabbed his gun-wrist, held it back so that Jackson was a helpless target for those in the rear.

Jackson's life hung in the balance, at that moment. Ram Singh had gone down, either shot or tripped by an obstacle he was hurdling. Wentworth could not possibly reach the car before his faithful chauffeur was killed and thrown from the running board. There was only one thing to do—and cold sweat trickled down Wentworth's spine as he made the split-second decision. He sighted his guns as he never had before.

Their roar was almost simultaneous, but not quite. The right-hand weapon barked a fractional second sooner than its mate. It sent a leaden slug whistling within a scant inch of Jackson's jugular, burying itself in the brain of the thug holding him. Almost paralleling that bullet sped one which brought a hoarse scream from the back of the car as it scythed down the killer already triggering the shot that would have ended Jackson's life.

The driver waited for no more. Desperately, he threw the car into gear and gassed it forward with a leap that sent Jackson spinning from the running board. Before Wentworth could fire again, it was out of range. He dived into a clump of bushes, as Jackson scrambled to his feet and looked around for his savior.

A nearby vault offered the cover Wentworth needed. Circling behind it, he worked his way toward a low, tree-crowned hill, then struck off at an angle, safe from pursuit and possible recognition.

Someone, he knew now, was not altogether certain that he was dead. Someone figured that he might be faking a burial, somehow allowing himself to be buried alive for a few hours and then disinterred when all watchers had gone. That someone had taken out grim death insurance to make sure that the body which went down into the grave would never come up alive.

No smallest chance that Richard Wentworth might live was being overlooked by this implacable enemy. As he realized the extent of the fiend's hatred, he shuddered—not for himself, but helpless Nita. Once more, he realized how important it was that he must stay dead until this criminal menace was wiped out. How perilous it would be for her if the master of the Sleeping Death should decide that he was still alive and determined to reach out for him—through the girl he loved.

THAT DISMAYING possibility was still torturing Wentworth when he turned the key in the door of Terry Trimble's apartment. But the moment the door opened he tensed, every nerve a-tingle, alert to meet the present danger. There was a light burning in the living room, and he recalled there had been none when he left. First, a light, now the creak of a chair, then the soft tinkle of an ash receiver....

Warily, gun in hand, Wentworth inched his way along the wall of the little reception hall, flung himself through the arched entrance to the protection of a heavy settee—then looked across the room to find Sylvia Lane sitting back in an easy chair, watching him with an amused smile.

His eyes flashed around the room, through the open door of the bedroom, the bath. Apparently, she was alone, but the automatic was still in readiness at his side as he strode lithely from one door to the other, investigating each room before turning back to her. She was alone, but his swift inspection convinced him that she had searched the apartment from end to end. Then he heard her voice.

"Nobody here but the two of us," she said, smiling, as he slipped the gun back into its holster and half-sat on the arm of the settee facing her. "It's very improper, I know—but I hope you won't mind. We can talk much better alone. I've wanted to talk to you, ever since the other night."

She was pretty, no doubt of that. From some angles the cameo quality of her profile made her fairly beautiful, and now she was turning it on for him—turning it on strong. She had other attractions, and knew it—her full bosom, artfully half-revealed by the negligent droop of her blouse, shapely legs, crossed so that he could not miss several inches of pink flesh above the top of one stocking.

"I liked the way you handled yourself the other night, Terry Trimble." She eyed him appreciatively, altogether unabashed at her intrusion. "That was nice work. That's why I am here—to make you a proposition. The chief—the man I work with, if you want to put it that way—can use a man like you. *I* can use you, too... if you will play my way."

"I'm listening," Wentworth said. "What's the proposition?"

"I don't know why you were there in Willis' apartment the other night," she said softly. "But the game could not have been worth your while. At best, you were playing for a piker's stake—and I'm talking *real* money, Trimble. I can contact you with the biggest thing that ever hit this man's town—"

"The Sleeping Death," Wentworth suggested.

"The Sleeping Death," she admitted blandly. "I am a member

of the organization that controls it. So was Willis, but he got cold feet and tried to squeal—and you saw what happened to him. We need another good man—not a Willis Fleming, but a man like Terry Trimble. You can have Fleming's place, Terry—not only with the chief—" she leaned forward so that the low-necked blouse fell away provokingly, and her dark eyes bored into his—"but with me."

What was the meaning of this surprising proposal? What did she really want with him? Did she take him for an average, none-too-scrupulous private detective, an adventurer always open to a proposition that sounded like easy money—or was there something more than that behind the pressure she was putting on him?

Wentworth tried to find the answers in the depths of her melting eyes. Now she was getting to her feet, flowing out of her chair with the sinuous glide of a cat rising from its sleeping cushion—was there at his side, the curves of her plush-soft body close against him. Her full red lips were parted, eyes half-closed, hands on his shoulders… and then she was in his arms, moist, eager lips closing over his in a kiss of complete yielding.

"You win, sister." Wentworth simulated a huskiness, an emotional response, which he was far from feeling as she drew away and looked up expectantly, waiting for his answer. "When do we begin?"

"Now," she beamed upon him. "I thought I read you right, Terry. I told the chief to expect you." She glanced at her watch. "He's waiting for us now."

As soon as they reached the street, she took command, led

67

him halfway down the block to where a limousine was standing at the curb. A liveried chauffeur ushered them in and then took his seat at the wheel, driving off without waiting for directions. Wentworth noted the route, saw that they had turned into Fifth Avenue, that they were headed uptown—but Sylvia Lane's arm was slipping around him, drawing him close.

"Until the chief has okayed you, I shall have to cover your eyes," she apologized softly as she drew his face down onto her breast and covered it with her handkerchief. He did not draw back from it.

The fragrance with which it was saturated was overpowering, fairly took his breath away; and, before Wentworth could resist, he felt his senses swimming, drifting off into a soft, luxurious contentment....

THE LIMOUSINE was in what looked like a garage— and smelled, he noted, like the garage of a hospital—when he regained full control of his senses. Sylvia Lane was standing outside the open door of the car, smiling, extending her soft hand to lead him to a recessed section at one side of the stone-walled room where a black-robed and masked figure waited.

The robe, Wentworth noted, covered him from neck to shoes. The mask was really a cowl. It fitted over his face tightly and then went back over his head and hung down to his shoulders. Even his eyes were shielded by what seemed to be panes of blue cellophane in the eye-slits of the mask—an excellent way of disguising their color.

"Miss Lane has told me about you, Trimble," he acknowledged, as soon as the girl had introduced her new recruit. "She seems to be considerably impressed with your qualifications, and I value her opinion. I need a man who is dependable, resourceful, fearless—who can direct and command and will give me implicit obedience."

He paused, waited expectantly, and Wentworth nodded.

"You seem to be the man I am looking for," came from behind the mask in a voice that the speaker very obviously was trying to disguise—but that Wentworth was almost certain he recognized. "I think I can use you. *But what were you doing in Willis Fleming's apartment Monday night?*"

The way that query was blurted at him was intended to take him by surprise. But Wentworth eyed those cellophane slits calmly and answered deliberately.

"That is my business—or, rather, the business of the client who employed me. I understood you to say that you expected dependability and trustworthiness in your men."

Sultry silence followed that refusal, and Wentworth tensed himself, ready for trouble—although he had already discovered that he had been relieved of his shoulder-holstered automatics while unconscious in the car. The eyes behind the cellophane panes fairly blazed at him, but then the "chief" seemed to think better of it. The hooded head nodded.

"A good answer," he conceded. "Give me the same loyalty, and you will be well repaid. I am going to accept you, Trimble. I am going to give you a chance to become a millionaire—a multi-millionaire. My men already have made fortunes, but this is only the beginning. I will not be satisfied until this city is paying a toll such as nobody has ever conceived. Not only this city—but Chicago, Philadelphia, Boston—every city in the nation. Every city, with one of my lieutenants in charge of the local organization, sending its tribute back to headquarters—back to us!"

A madman's dream, Wentworth mentally catalogued the man's raving—a crazy dream, appallingly dangerous. It had already cost hundreds of lives and might run its ghastly toll into the thousands unless this fellow was checked.

Keenly, he watched the man as he listened—filing away in his mind observations that set his pulse beating faster. The cut of those shoulders, the way the head was carried—all so familiar. The way the right foot kept tapping on the floor, the hands were behind the back. Wentworth could see them continually moving, twitching....

"You will join us tonight," the poorly-disguised voice was saying. "One of my men will call for you at your apartment at about eight-thirty."

That was his dismissal, the signal for Sylvia Lane to lead him back to the limousine and squeeze his hand significantly as she promised to see him that evening. The moment the door closed, Wentworth again smelled that overpowering fragrance, felt his senses reeling. But as he slipped into unconsciousness he smiled to himself—for he was practically certain that the masked chief was none other than Dr. Emil Anderson!

WHEN THOUSANDS SLEPT IN HELL

CHAPTER 6
BULLET BALLET

A NDERSON WAS the head of the criminal outfit and the Morellis were his assistants. Wentworth decided this, as he reviewed his observations after the limousine had delivered him, fully recovered, to the door of his apartment. Perhaps it was through the unethical Doc Roth that the hookup between the two had been made. At any rate, now it was an accomplished fact—a deadly combination that united that perverted power of modern science with the widespread organization of the underworld. This combination he must smash at any cost!

The afternoon papers, brought in from a newsstand, were filled with the latest depredations of the Sleeping Death. New victims were added to the ever-lengthening list, and again the *Enquirer* man had contacted additional anonymous tribute-payers. He estimated that the number of those keeping silent, and paying tribute, ran high in the hundreds—the extortion money they already had yielded was far in excess of a million! It staggered him.

There was also a statement from the harried police commissioner.

"The police are investigating important developments in the so-called Sleeping Death cases," Commissioner Kirkpatrick announced. "From evidence now in our possession, it is safe to predict arrests within the next twenty-four hours which will put an end to this menace. It is of paramount importance, however, that the public refuse to allow themselves to be stampeded into the panic which the perpetrators of these outrages desire."

Wentworth had read statements like this before. He could visualize Stanley Kirkpatrick, at his wit's end, hoping against hope for a break that would crack the case—at the same time vainly striving to avert the terrified panic sweeping down on the city. When a man of Kirkpatrick's sagacity and experience made a pathetic bid for twenty-four hours of grace, the situation must be desperate.

Once more, Wentworth realized, the greatest police force in the world was confronted by a criminal menace against which it was helpless—a savage menace that would not only loot but enslave the prostrate city unless the Spider succeeded in destroying it....

Wentworth was ready when the apartment buzzer summoned him at eight-thirty—prepared for anything. An olive-skinned youth, in his early twenties, stood in the hall when Wentworth opened the door warily.

"Okay, Trimble," the guide grinned. "We're waiting for you. Needn't hang onto that gat." He nodded to the coat pocket where Wentworth's fingers were closed on the butt of an automatic. "You're okay with us. If the boss wanted you drilled, I coulda' done it a dozen times while you were yappin' with him this afternoon."

He led the way to where a large sedan waited at the corner with three other men besides the driver. One of these was introduced to him as Clip Dugan, squad leader.

"You got your gats, ain't you?" Dugan demanded. "You're

gonna have the chance to use them. Now just watch me. When I start blastin', you back me up. This joint we're goin' to—we're gonna scare hell outta them, see? Just bang away like it's the Fourth o' July—the more racket the better."

The "joint" was in the theatrical district, it appeared, when the car headed into the West Fifties and rolled into a parking lot.

"All set now." Dugan took the lead, as they walked out to the street. "Just take it easy. Remember—" he smirked—"you're goin' to a show!"

Curiously Wentworth watched the theaters and nightclubs they passed, speculating on which would be their destination. Then he blinked with surprise. They were going into the Yankee Music Hall—the establishment operated by Hammer Gunther and Jessie Ogilvie! It was more than coincidence, he knew instantly. In some way this visit tied up with that set-to that had occurred outside Willis Fleming's apartment house. But how? By Sylvia Lane's admission, this gang had murdered young Fleming; and Hammer Gunther and his female companion had next jumped Wentworth in order to free Doretta Cahill and Sam Pavvy, the pair who had robbed Fleming's safe.

Something about that set-up was all haywire; it just didn't make sense. But there was an even greater surprise in store for Wentworth when Dugan herded him inside with the others....

THE PERFORMANCE had not yet begun, but the hall was well-filled, the spectators grouped around round tables instead of seated in the usual theater fashion. An usher led them to their reservation, but Wentworth noticed that Dugan's eyes

In less than a minute, the hall had been transformed from a place of entertainment into a ghastly hell!

were darting about the audience. The squad leader was nodding his head, twisting his face in covert signals.

"Looks like we're all here," Dugan said softly, as he slid onto his chair. "Happy's over there on the left. Jake's on the right—an' I think that's Louie's bunch up there near the stage."

If those three other leaders each had five men, as Dugan did, it meant there were at least twenty-four of the gang scattered through the audience. Leaning back in his chair, to spot them— he found himself staring at Doretta Cahill and Sam Pavvy!

What they were doing in Hammer Gunther's music hall was more than he could hope to figure out....

The girl was ill at ease. Her fingers were rubbing the tabletop, and she kept looking around as if searching for someone. Pavvy, on the other hand, seemed enjoying himself hugely. A glass of beer in one hand, sandwich in the other, he was the picture of satisfaction.

Wentworth's observation was cut short when the lights went out, and the curtain rose. The production, a musical melodrama, with a gaslight period chorus alternating with the dramatic cast, was utterly wasted on Clip Dugan. He sat tensely on the edge of his chair, not even looking at the stage but expectantly wait- ing, listening....

In the middle of a ballet number, Wentworth caught the signal.

Down front, near the stage, an argument had started. A disgruntled drunkard, creating a disturbance, it seemed at first. Then sounded two angry voices, a third—and, with a crash of breaking glasses, a table was overturned. Women screamed, men got to their feet, the chorus tried to ignore the commotion as waiters swarmed through the hall... then Clip Dugan leaned across the table.

"Cut loose!" His weapon was out, barking thunderously as he sprang to his feet.

That shot was echoed by a dozen from all parts of the house—shots that were not being fired into the air, Wentworth noted grimly, as he saw waiters going down on all sides. Every one of those bullets was finding a mark, either in one of the hall's employees or a terrified patron trying vainly to scramble out of the roaring bedlam. Just in time, Wentworth ducked out of the way, half-tumbled over a table as he glimpsed the olive-skinned youth drawing down on him.

The bullet barely missed Wentworth and drilled the throat of another man with a gun in his hand. That shot might have been a mistake, but there was no time to hold an inquest. Springing to his feet, Wentworth leaped silently… and his gun barrel smashed through the young killer's skull!

A heavy-set, thick-jowled man came out onto the stage from which the terrified chorines had fled screaming. It was Hammer Gunther. He raised his arms, tried to still the pandemonium… and a dozen bullets seemed to strike him at once. They fairly blasted him back against the garish scenery, a corpse before he hit the floor.

The hall had been transformed from a place of carefree entertainment into a ghastly hell. Sick with horror, Wentworth saw the senseless carnage all around him. A question shrieked in his brain—why this wanton slaughter of innocent people? Simply because Hammer Gunther and his partner refused to pay the tribute the ruthless master of the Sleeping Death demanded? Was this another horrible example staged as a warning to those who might disobey him?

Such savagery seemed incredible. There *must* be something

more to it! Then Wentworth saw that something had gone wrong. Two of Dugan's men were down. The thunder of guns was louder, had a new note. It was the unmistakable chatter of a tommy gun! No doubt about it.

"Damn the double-crossing rats!" Dugan swore as he dived to cover.

Decidedly, something had gone wrong. The members of the gang were retreating toward Dugan's corner. Other grim-faced killers were pressing behind, cutting them down as mercilessly as they had slaughtered waiters and bystanders!

WENTWORTH HAD been doing his best to help the terrified guests escape. Now he was forced to take refuge behind an upturned table like the others. These newcomers, he noticed, were charging right across the spot where Doretta Cahill had been sitting—where she must be now. Sam Pavvy rose from behind a table—and went down with a row of tommy-gun bullets through his skull. If Pavvy was still there, the girl must also be on the floor....

Wentworth shifted his position, started toward her—and a bullet split the table beside his head, just as he ducked out of the path of a fear-crazed man running blindly through the shambles. That bullet had come from behind!

Wentworth whirled. The savage killer's lust in the beady eyes of Clip Dugan was unmistakable. The lip was curled back over his teeth in a snarl, finger tightening again on the trigger. Before he could fire, he pitched forward—one of Wentworth's bullets in his brain.

So that was it! The place was a death-trap into which Wentworth had been led for slaughter. First, the olive-skinned killer and then Dugan had tried to carry out their orders—orders from the chief and certainly known to Sylvia Lane....

Was Doretta Cahill another of the lambs decoyed here for slaughter? It seemed likely. Perhaps the girl was dead already. Then he saw her. In some miraculous way, she had gotten out of the line of fire. Now she was wandering through the panic-stricken crowd that jammed all the doors, trying ineffectually to find a way out.

Wentworth reached her just as two thugs started dragging her to one side of the hall. One fired at him point-blank—and if his gun had not jammed the Spider's career would have ended on the spot. Wentworth smashed his gun into the killer's face, then whirled to cut down his partner before that surprised thug had the chance to release the girl.

Freed, Doretta Cahill fled. Before Wentworth caught up with her, she was out of the main hall, fighting her way to the rooms beyond—kitchen, pantries, wardrobe, the office. From one to the other she raced, tugging doors open, searching in a wild frenzy.

Twice Wentworth tried to get her to leave with him, but she hardly seemed to hear. Brushing him aside, she ran past to the next room, the next. Mystified, he followed her... until he caught the ominous tang of smoke!

The place was on fire. A glance into the wrecked hall revealed red tongues licking up the side of one wall, spreading like a pot of brilliant red paint spilled on a floor. That old building would be consumed like cardboard. There was not a moment to lose—

she *must* leave. But even then she struggled wildly to break away when he seized her.

"You can't stay here!" he shouted. "You'll roast to death!"

But fire seemed to have no terror for her. She was babbling something about "that woman."

"I've got to find her—don't you understand? She was here! If I can't find her, at least I can find where she hid it! I've got to, no matter what happens—"

Wentworth saw that she was hysterical. But suddenly her eyes cleared magically—then flooded with the wild terror of a trapped fugitive. Frenziedly, she clutched his lapels.

"Get me out!" she begged. "Don't let them take me! I can't let them arrest me!"

Now he understood. It was the shrill sound of police whistles that had brought her back to rationality. The police were out there in the wrecked hall, mopping up what was left of the battle. Her only desire was to get away from them.

"I think there's a way out the back," he told her. "Past the kitchen. There should be a driveway there."

She was already running toward it. Wentworth followed, dashing through the kitchen and down a short hallway. She was tugging frantically at the door when he reached her and got it open. Beyond was the unrelieved blackness of an unlighted alley, a service entrance utterly still and dark after the howling nightmare just left.

For a moment, the girl clung to him, frightened by the darkness. Then he led the way, the door closed behind them—and he blundered straight into the hands of men who converged on him from every side. Doretta Cahill screamed, an abortive scream that was strangled almost the instant it left her lips. Then he knew that she was beside him, dragged along through the darkness, pitched into the back of a car, pinned helplessly on the floor.

The powerful motor sprang to life, and the car was underway, out of the alley, into the street. Wentworth could hear the noises of New York's night life all around him—laughing voices, honking horns, shrilling traffic whistles—but the cold muzzle of an automatic, ground against his temple, discouraged any attempt to call for help. The girl shook with terror as a gloved hand was clamped tight over her mouth.

Not until they were out of the theater district, in the deserted quiet of midtown, did Wentworth have an opportunity to identify their captors. In the light of a passing arc-lamp, he glimpsed the man gagging the girl—Vic Morelli.

But the same light that enabled him to see Morelli betrayed him as well. Suddenly the automatic at his temple jerked away. His head was grabbed, twisted around, face upward.

"Geez!" Tony Morelli swore wrathfully. "This ain't the feller! I never seen this punk! He's put somethin' over on us!"

Murder flared poisonously in his eyes, and Wentworth momentarily expected to feel the searing agony of a leaden slug ripping through his gullet. But Vic Morelli ruled otherwise.

"If he ain't the guy, we can use him anyway," he decided as he took hold of his brother's wrist and turned the gun away. "He was with her, wasn't he? Maybe she won't enjoy hearin' him howl, if she tries givin' us a stall—and refuses to take us to the real gent you want!"

CHAPTER 7
HELL'S HOTEL

TONY MORELLI'S pudgy face twisted into a malicious snarl. His dark eyes gleamed with evil anticipation as he hovered over his prisoner, jabbing the gun muzzle painfully into Wentworth's neck. As he lay there, Wentworth wondered who it was they could want so badly. Was it Sam Pavvy? The safecracker was of no importance, a nobody in the criminal world—surely, he was not worth all this trouble. And yet Pavvy was the man who had been with Doretta Cahill in the music hall....

His speculation ended abruptly when the car came to a halt on a lonely block near the East River. Somewhere in the Thirties, Wentworth judged it to be—a neighborhood abandoned even by the impoverished families who once had dwelled there. A block of stores, long without customers; buildings almost tenantless.

The house before which they had stopped was desolate. The windows of the stores on the first floor were boarded up, the upper floors gaping hollowly through broken panes and sagging sashes. The door was secured by a padlock, but Tony Morelli had the key. He led the way with a flashlight, while his brother and two men followed with the captives.

Through a musty, plaster-littered hallway, down a flight of

rickety steps to a dank, rodent-infested cellar they were dragged. Tony Morelli already had lighted two thick plumber's candles stuck in wrecks of lanterns hanging from the ceiling. Now, like a medieval torturer, he stood waiting for his victims.

Wentworth tried to make a break, tripped one of the men who held him, dropped to the floor. But they were on him in a flash, stunning him with a smash over the head from a revolver butt. Before he had come out of the daze, he was tied up helplessly against a rusty iron pillar.

Doretta Cahill's stifled scream brought him out of the semi-conscious coma. She was directly in front of him, not a dozen feet away, held securely by Vic Morelli. He had her elbows pinioned. Her face was tear-stained, eyes were wide with pain and terror as she tried to shrink away. Tony's fingers fastened around her ear, gripping it in a cruel vise.

"Where is he?" he rasped, face close against hers. "Where's the Doc? Maybe he can hide out from the cops, but *we're* gonna find him. Talk, damn you—talk!"

His fingers tightened on her ear, mercilessly. Her mouth was open, sobbing out a weak moan of agony, but not a word of information came. That torturing grip twisted and twisted, until Wentworth expected to see the ear torn off her head.

Hopelessly, he cursed them. Now he noticed half a dozen newcomers, members of the gang who must have arrived while he was unconscious. Wide-eyed, they watched, chuckling bestially and urging Tony on to his further excesses.

But the girl had reached the end of her endurance. The moan

died on her lips; her eyes closed. Disgustedly, Tony released his grip as her cheek fell limply against his knotted fingers.

"She'll talk," he gritted savagely, as they held her head back and forced raw-smelling whisky into her mouth. "She'll talk if I hafta' take her apart!"

Out of his pocket he took a cigarette, lit it and puffed until the coal burned red.

"Rip open her dress," he ordered as Doretta came back to gagging consciousness. "I'll give her a taste of hell."

Eagerly, his fellows ran forward to obey. But again it was Vic Morelli who stopped them.

"Not on the girl," he insisted. "Burns will show. If the cops ever get hold o' you, you'll sweat blood for it. Yeah, I know, we're not gonna be caught. But just in case somethin' should slip, I'm not gonna have any girl provin' torture against me. That's bad business on women. If you wanna use the fire, go to work on her boyfriend."

Regretfully, Tony moved away. But the glare he turned on Wentworth promised full satisfaction for his frustration. Grabbing one of Wentworth's bound arms, he twisted it up from the elbow, held it there—and jammed the cherry coal of the cigarette against the captive's fist, pressing it down between the middle fingers....

Hellishly it burned, first a stabbing sword then like hungry teeth eating into the flesh, Wentworth kept that fist clenched as long as he possibly could... then he had to spread his fingers, and the hot coal bit into the tender skin beneath them. Grimly, he clenched his teeth, while the odor of his burning flesh filled his nostrils, beads of perspiration trickling down his face. Opposite, the girl watched with wide, staring eyes, face contorted into a mask of utter horror, mouth half-open as if to utter a scream that would not come.

"That's only a sample," Tony promised tauntingly, "only the beginning. After I'm finished workin' on your hands, I'll try under your arms. Then your belly...."

The half-extinguished cigarette was again between his lips, kindling red again as he puffed it. He grabbed Wentworth's throbbing hand—but now the girl could watch no more.

"No—no!" she shrieked. "Don't burn him—he doesn't know anything about it. Don't, I tell you!" as Morelli again ground the glowing ash against the captive fist. "I'll talk! I'll tell you anything—I'll take you there! I'll show you where he is! I can't let you do *that!*"

Like a swarm of bees they were around her, firing questions, demanding proof that she was not lying.

"He's at the Kenilworth Arms," she repeated the name of a fashionable apartment hotel. "I'll go with you—that's the only way you can get in. If I'm lying, you can do anything you want to me."

Satisfied at last, the Morellis cut Wentworth loose and loaded them into the back of the car again.

AS THEY sped across town, Wentworth's brain was again striving to fathom the mystery that seemed to become increasingly baffling. He had been certain that the Morellis were hand-in-glove with Anderson—with the master of the Sleeping Death. What other explanation could there be for Tony's murderous attack on him and Nita? And yet, here they were kidnapping Anderson's nurse and forcing her to take them to the refuge where George Holden, one of Anderson's employees, was hiding out, a fugitive from the law for the murder of Eugene Fajans—*who had been a victim of the Sleeping Death!*

It was simply running around in a circle, getting nowhere.

Another thing, he had recognized several of these thugs as Morelli's men who had taken part in the battle of the Music Hall—members of that charging band of killers who had shot down the "chief's" men. Why had they done that? The whole thing just didn't make sense....

"There's the dump down the street," Tony announced, peering between the men on the front seat. "Okay, Pete, drive right up to the front. I'll take care of the admiral."

The "admiral," waiting at the curb, opened the sedan door courteously—and froze as Tony's gun was jammed into his face. Like an automaton, he pivoted at the gangster's command, and marched into the lobby—a perfect screen for the thugs behind him. Before the night clerk could move from the desk, he was overpowered. Then, one after the other, the two elevator men were taken in charge the moment they brought their cars to the ground floor.

"Solly, you hop behind the desk and keep a gun on this guy," Tony ordered swiftly. "The first thing he tries, let him have it. Pooch, you take the admiral into that elevator and run it up to the roof. See that he and that monkey in the car don't bother us for a while. The rest of you hop into the other car."

Swiftly, without a hitch—without the slightest chance for

Wentworth to make an attempt to escape—the thing was accomplished. In little more than a minute, they were crowded into an elevator and going up to the eighteenth floor—surging down the hallway, dragging the white-faced, trembling operator with them.

Pale and tight-lipped, as if going to her death, Doretta Cahill led the way to an apartment door and rang the buzzer. There was no response.

"There's somebody in there!" Tony cursed obscenely. "I heard him moving. He's wise—or this dame's givin' him the office to scram!"

"No—no!" the girl protested, then, as she pressed the buzzer again, put her mouth close to the door. "George, it's Doretta," she called. "Open the door—please, George!"

Not a sound from within—but Tony Morelli was waiting no longer. Pushing her aside, he blazed away at the lock, put half a dozen bullets into it that drilled and splintered the door. When he stepped aside, two of his huskies hurled themselves at the door, and the lock tore from its weakened frame.

The door flew open, and the charging men, unable to stop themselves, catapulted through the inside hallway—when a blast of machine-gun fire hurled them back on their heels!

"He's out there on the fire escape—with a tommy!" Tony howled, flinging himself to one side of the doorway.

Unhindered, the door slammed shut. They could hear the last of that withering blast thudding into its inner side. After that, silence... utter silence.

For long minutes they crouched there before daring to open

that door. Then Tony Morelli pushed it back slowly with a fire-ax one of his men had found on the wall. Not a sound greeted this maneuver. On hands and knees, Morelli crawled over the threshold, past the bullet-riddled bodies of his men, to the door of the living room.

"He's gone—the joint's empty," he called back to those behind him.

Instantly his words were belied. From one of the other rooms came a moan of agony! It filled their ears with sound.

Tony Morelli was the first one into the room, a bedchamber off the living room. He dropped to his knees, lifting the blood-drenched form of a dying man into his arms.

"Who done it to you, Doc? Who done it to you?" he pleaded as he tried to shake an answer out of the near-corpse.

Doc Roth was literally shot to pieces. Blood streamed from more than a dozen bullet wounds, but he rallied sufficiently to force words from his dying lips.

"Anderson… Doc Anderson!" he gasped. "He got me as soon as I came in… tommy gun! He jumped me from… next door…."

The last few words were hardly intelligible, a mere whisper. Then his head rolled to one side, dead.

"Next door," Vic Morelli repeated. "That's how the louse got him—from the apartment next door!"

Galvanized into action by his own words, he leaped across the bedroom to a door connecting the apartment beyond. It was locked, but he quickly followed his brother's example. His gun splintered the wood, shattered the lock, and his charging bulk sent the door flying inward.

More cautious than the two who had died in the blast of tommy-gun fire, he caught the sides of the doorway as he charged, held himself there. His face convulsed with horror, eyes fairly bulging out as he stared into the next room. An elderly man and his wife sat there, apparently peacefully sleeping in their chairs. Sleeping through all that din? They were dead!

"The Sleeping Death!" Tony gasped as he staggered back, ashen-faced. "God-a'mighty—he gave it to this dump! He figured we'd come here—so he fixed it so we'd stumble into it an' get a whiff of it ourselves!"

The Sleeping Death! As if it were the Black Plague, they turned and ran; fought with one another to get through the doorway and race to the elevator. Wentworth and Doretta Cahill were forgotten. Nothing mattered but to get away before they, too, were stricken.

AS SOON as they were gone, Wentworth closed the door to the adjoining apartment and then quickly searched the one in which George Holden had been living. Holden's clothing was still in the closets, his personal effects around the place, but the pathologist was gone.

He remembered Doretta Cahill, but figured it was more important to find the killer.

Running to the window from which that submachine gun blast had come, Wentworth found that there was no fire escape. However, a length of rope still dangled from the edge of the roof and told how the killer had escaped—George Holden with him. Wentworth ran out into the hall and located the stairwell, dashed up the two flights to the roof, and stepped out into the faintly starlit darkness.

In the deeper shadows of the roof-house, he waited to accustom his eyes to the blackness. He was certain he heard the sound of roofing sagging under footsteps. Cautiously, he crept forward—then threw himself flat as a fusillade of shots stabbed out at him. From what seemed half a dozen points, orange flashes spurted, and lead whistled close to his head.

Unarmed since the Morellis took his guns, Wentworth was helpless against this number—could only lie there and hope the killers would figure he was dead. Fortunately, they did not bother to investigate. He saw dark forms diving into the roof-house—how many he could not be certain. They clattered down the stairs, accomplishing an escape he could not hope to prevent.

He hurried back to the doorway and downstairs. What had those men been doing on the roof? Anderson and Holden would have had ample time to escape before this. These men must have had some other mission here—to do what?

To spread the Sleeping Death?

Suddenly he remembered that, with all the shooting and uproar, not a tenant had come from any of the other apartments to investigate. Not a soul had appeared in the corridors. Why?

Because they were all dead! Because the whole hotel had been stricken with the Sleeping Death!

That explained why the Morellis had taken to their heels so precipitately. They realized that doom had descended not only on the apartment next to Holden's but on all the others as well! Wentworth ran from apartment to apartment on the top floor, pounding on door after door… but not a soul answered. Back to the eighteenth floor, he rushed—to Holden's deserted apartment where he could grab the telephone and call the office.

There was no response—the telephone operators had died like the others!

The place had become a hotel of the dead, a ghastly hostelry in which he was the only living soul. He and Doretta Cahill… but now she was gone, too. She had taken advantage of his absence to make her escape—unless, like the others, she had also fallen a victim to the Sleeping Death….

Back in the corridor, Wentworth thumbed the elevator signal. The indicator hands did not budge; the cars were anchored on the ground floor. Down flight after flight, he raced. In the lobby, two policemen from a radio car had just arrived, summoned by tenants who had come in and found the elevator operators unconscious, slugged.

"The whole building—they're all dead!" Wentworth broke his appalling news. "Dead in their rooms—the Sleeping Death!"

He led the way to the switchboard room—and there, as he had feared, were both operators, slumped in their chairs, sleeping the sleep of death. Gently, he lifted one to the floor, took her place, plugged in connection after connection. Not an answering murmur came over the wires. One more call, and he turned to the wide-eyed policeman gaping helplessly in the doorway.

"There's headquarters," he snapped. "Make your report. I'm going through the building to see if anything can be done."

ARMED WITH rings of passkeys, he went from apartment to apartment, and Death leered at him each time he opened a door. Like the citizens of ancient Pompeii, caught by Vesuvius' lava, the guests of the Kenilworth Arms had been arrested in the midst of their normal activities, caught in mid-operation, lulled into the long, fatal sleep.

Not until the building had been searched from top to bottom was the full extent of that fearful tragedy known. Throughout those twenty floors Death had set its seal. Of the hundreds of souls who had tenanted it a short while before, only four were still alive—the desk clerk, doorman and two elevator operators—only those and the ones who had been in George Holden's hideout apartment....

George Holden, Dr. Anderson and Doc Roth—Wentworth tried to reconstruct what had transpired in that apartment between the three men.

In some way, Doc Roth had discovered that Holden was hiding there. Was it his call that had made Holden summon Dr. Anderson and the Sleeping Death? No, because Roth had said that Anderson "got him" as soon as he came in. That meant that Anderson had been there with Holden. Together they must have planned that ghastly hotel slaughter, perhaps had already perpetrated it before Roth arrived!

Doretta Cahill knew about that hideout apartment, Wentworth considered, as he slipped away before the police had a chance to drag him to headquarters for a cross-examining he did not dare face. She knew about that apartment and had stood tight-lipped, through agonizing torture, rather than lead the way there. She had purposely given the ghastly Sleeping Death time to do its work. Of all the hotel guests only George Holden had escaped—the man she loved. Yet, despite this damning evidence arrayed against her, Wentworth could not conceive of her in the murder role she seemed to be playing....

But he was hardly back to Terry Trimble's apartment when all thought of Doretta Cahill was wiped abruptly from his mind. He hardly had sat down to ponder the night's tragic events, when the telephone rang. Dr. Rogers' voice, grave with concern, came to him over the wire the moment he picked up the receiver.

"I've been trying to get you all evening, Wentworth," he said anxiously. "It's about Miss van Sloan—her condition has taken a serious turn for the worse. You had better come here at once. I'm afraid—afraid of what may develop...."

CHAPTER 8
INTO THE SHADOWS

NITA WAS dying... Nita was dying! That terrible thought pounded through Richard Wentworth's brain, as he crouched on the edge of a cab seat and pleaded with the driver to make better time to the Calvin Memorial Hospital. Nita was dying. Nothing less would have induced Dr. Rogers to speak as he had. Nita might be dead even before he arrived!

A paroxysm of stark agony stabbed through him at the thought of her death—at the terrifying thought of long, meaningless days and nights without her... of a life that would lose all savor and purpose. There *would* be no life for him without

Nita—there *could* be none. She was part of him—his inspiration, comfort, constant companion even when he was not with her....

The cab seemed fairly to creep. A dozen times he felt that he could stand the waiting no longer; that he must leap out and run the rest of the way. But at last he was racing up the hospital steps, looking into the physician's worried face—and his heart sank like a stone.

"She is very ill, Wentworth." The medico shook his head gravely. "She has been losing ground all day. I can't say why, except that she seems to have no desire to live. I am doing all that I can for her—but she doesn't seem to be trying to help herself."

"I can see her?" Wentworth's voice had difficulty coming out of his throat. "That will be all right?"

"Yes," Rogers nodded. "In fact, I want you to. The way she has been sinking, I think she will reach the crisis tonight. When that time comes, I want you to be with her."

The palms of Wentworth's hands were moist, cold; a sharp lump formed in his throat as he opened the door of the private room to which the physician led him. Hesitantly, he stepped inside and glanced with an awe that was almost reverential at the white-sheeted bed—the pale face lying on the pillow.

Cold fingers closed around his heart, seemed to drain it of all blood, as he saw how thin and unearthly pale her face had become. Her lovely coloring had gone, been replaced with an ethereal quality that did not belong to this world....

Wentworth's knees trembled with a sudden fright such as no jeopardy to his own life ever had been able to give him, as he started toward the bed. A huge Great Dane at the bedside rose

and bristled suspiciously. A low rumble started from its throat—
and then Apollo, Nita's statuesque pet, wagged his tail in recognition as his keen animal senses penetrated the disguise which
would have deceived the sharpest eyes of mere men.

Gently, Wentworth patted the dog's head, and the faithful
guardian sank back to the floor to resume his vigil.

Nita's eyes had been closed when Wentworth came into the
room, but now they were open, looking at him but not seeing
him. As he gazed into their violet depths, he saw that she was
looking past him, into scenes which she alone could see... scenes
which terrified her.

"Get those things off, Dick!" she whispered suddenly. "They're
coming—the police! They mustn't find you like that! Hurry,—
let me help... Oh, I can't get it off! There won't be time. Roll
over, quick! Rub your face in the dirt... that will help!—it will
have to do!"

Her mind was wandering, he realized as he listened—and a
chill ran up his spine. Her mind was wandering with *him*—with
the Spider—reliving a time she had barely managed to get him
out of the telltale makeup to save him from recognition by the
police.

"Down, Dick! Down on the floor!" she gasped as she half-sat
up in bed. "Crawl out to me while I hold them off. Here, take
this mask...."

That was the time she had snatched him out of Stanley Kirkpatrick's office by flooding it with gas just as he was about to
be led off to jail. In her delirium, she was enduring again all the

NITA VAN SLOAN

96

perils gone through with him, suffering all the hours of unendurable waiting he had caused her.

HER UNCONSCIOUS words stabbed into his heart, twisted in the wounds of self-recrimination they inflicted. But it was worse when her tone changed, when she sank back onto the pillow, her voice soft and filled with pathetic longing.

"Burma… Ceylon… India," she whispered. "Romantic lands… peaceful lands."

"Nita!" Wentworth took her hands and pressed close to her. "Nita, darling—listen to me! We'll go to those peaceful lands— I'll take you there. Just get well and strong—"

She was looking right at him, but there was no recognition.

"Nita!" he tried again. "It's Dick, darling. Don't you know me? Don't you recognize—"

But, of course, she didn't! How could he expect her befogged eyes to penetrate his makeup? Quickly, he went to work, stripping off every vestige of Terry Trimble, restoring Richard Wentworth as she knew and loved him. Now his arms went around her, held her close.

"Please, Nita," he begged. "Look at me, darling. Look at me and listen. I am here with you now. Dick is here—sitting with you, holding you in his arms."

97

Gradually, the filmy curtain of the faraway began to fade from her eyes. Recognition was beginning to dawn in them.

"Dick," she whispered. "Dick... Dick...."

Slowly, she came back to full consciousness, complete rationality, and a flood of unbelieving happiness drowned the surprise in her eyes. She spoke softly now.

"I thought that you were dead," she whispered. "You never came to see me. When I asked for you, they made excuses—excuses that I couldn't believe because they weren't like you. I thought that they killed you, too, after you got out of the car that awful night—"

"I had to let you believe that, darling," he soothed. "I wanted everyone to believe that—especially the ones who did this to you. But that's all over now. All I want you to do is to get well enough so that I can take you away somewhere where there is peace and quiet and I can take care of you."

She was smiling wanly, happily—when suddenly her eyes filled with terror and her fingers gripped his convulsively. Wide-eyed, she stared at the door of the room. Wentworth whirled, saw that it had been opened—was just closing. In the narrowing aperture, he caught a glimpse of a young woman in a familiar dress.

Was she Doretta Cahill or Sylvia Lane? He didn't know, but whoever she was, she had been peering into the room—and had seen him in his actual guise! The moment that realization registered, he ran to the door and pulled it open. The corridor was empty—as quiet and empty as if the woman had never existed.

The moment he turned back to the bed he saw that Nita had

again lapsed into unconsciousness, and when he grasped her wrist, he could barely feel her pulse. Quickly, he called for Dr. Rogers, stood by anxiously while the physician worked over her silently and tensely. But there seemed to be no reaction to his efforts, no spark of animation in her graying cheeks.

Puzzled, baffled, Rogers stood back—and the slump of his shoulders, the evasion of his eyes, were their own admission of defeat.

Nita was dying!

Frantically, Wentworth took her in his arms, pressed his lips to her ear as he begged and pleaded with her—held her close as if to infuse his own strength into her stricken body.

"You *can't* leave me, darling—you *can't* go away!" he told her again and again—begging, pleading, concentrating all his will power on reaching her, probing deep down to her consciousness.

Her eyelids flickered, a half-sigh came from her lips—and Wentworth seized that wisp of returning life. By sheer will power, he clung to it, fanned it and kept it alive until a hint of color came back into her cheeks, until the beat of her heart became stronger and her breathing almost normal. There was a faint smile on her lips, and she dozed off into sleep.

"That is all," Rogers' voice spoke softly at his ear, and the physician's fingers squeezed his shoulder. "She has passed the crisis. You can go now. What she needs most is sleep."

GENTLY WENTWORTH drew his arm away from beneath her and rose from the bedside, still dazed from the ordeal through which he had just passed. He could go now, Rogers had said. Go—but go to what? It was no mere figment of the imagination that had given Nita that almost fatal scare. There *had* been someone outside that door. As he worked with his makeup kit, restoring the likeness of Terry Trimble, he wondered what had prompted that eavesdropper—what would await him once he left that room.

That question was answered the moment he stepped out into the corridor. Before his hand had left the knob of Nita's closing door, a white-uniformed attendant stepped up to him—and Wentworth felt the muzzle of a gun jammed into his ribs.

"The stairs at the end of the hall," his guide clipped.

Wentworth saw two more attendants waiting for him. From the corner of his eye, he glimpsed two others closing in from the rear. He was pocketed, trapped from all sides, but, worse than that, helpless because of Nita. Any disturbance—the blast of a shot or the uproar of a tussle might startle her out of her so necessary sleep. The shock would prove fatal.

Docilely, he walked the length of the hallway, and silently prayed that no nurse or doctor would appear and precipitate trouble. With a sigh of relief, he turned into the stairwell, saw the door close behind his captors, and started down to the street. Two of the pseudo-attendants had him by the arms now, offering no opportunity for escape—which was just what he wanted.

One flight down, another. The next would bring them to the street level—but halfway down he suddenly seemed to go weak at the knees. His legs doubled up beneath him and his arms wrapped around his stomach as he bent forward like a sufferer in the throes of agonizing cramps. That contortion was so swift, unexpected, that it took his guards completely by surprise. Unable to free their hands from his tightly locked arms, they were thrown forward, lost balance and pitched headfirst down the stairs.

Wentworth was after them instantly, taking steps three at a time as he dodged the bullets that blazed at him from those in the rear. In the tumble, one of the disguised thugs had dropped his gun. Wentworth snatched it up on the run, whirled and sent three shots up at his pursuers, slashed the barrel down on the skull of one of the fallen men who tried to grab him around the legs, and then sped down the remaining steps through a doorway at the foot of the flight.

The room beyond that doorway was the autopsy room, he saw at a glance. It was empty, except for a dozen high, white, enamel-topped tables with their ghastly burdens. On half of these were naked cadavers, already disemboweled or awaiting the pathologist's knife. On three lay corpses still covered with the sheets that had come with them from the morgue. Two others were unoccupied....

Instantly, he made his decision. Snatching the loose sheet from one of the covered bodies, he flung himself onto one of the empty tables, drew the cloth up over him and lay perfectly still.

Even before his body was completely relaxed, the thugs were after him, bursting into the room. The sight of those gruesome cadavers checked them at the doorway until one, who seemed to be their leader, stormed in after them.

"What are you standing here for?" he howled. "Afraid of harmless stiffs? While you stand gaping, he's getting away.

Through that back door—where else could he have gone? Get him or—"

They did not wait to hear his threat. Spurred on by the contempt in his tone, they raced between the rows of still figures, dived through the door he indicated. Within inches of Wentworth, they passed. Now he dared move his head, peer beneath the edge of the sheet—just in time to see the white-uniformed Dr. Emil Anderson raging after the thugs!

The moment the door closed behind Anderson, Wentworth sprang from the table, disentangled himself from the sheet and ran back the way he had come. Past the staircase and down a corridor opposite the autopsy room, he sped. Without further hindrance, he found his way to the front of the hospital, hurried down the steps and hailed a taxi. And now a new fear rode him.

That woman he had seen peering in at him through the doorway of Nita's room—if it actually was a woman, he believed... Had she recognized him as Richard Wentworth? If she had, his masquerade was now useless—and Nita's peril was even greater than before....

Was that woman's recognition the reason for this attack on him, or had he simply been tracked to the hospital and ambushed because of his interference with the master of the Sleeping Death? He could only pray that that was the solution—pray, and meanwhile plan a little chat with the eminent Dr. Anderson. But before he was ready for that interview he must return to the Trimble apartment for ammunition and automatics to replace those the Morellis had taken from him.

AGAIN, THE moment he let himself into the apartment,

he knew that someone else had been there. He knew it by the odor of Turkish cigarette smoke in the air, by the butts ground out in the ash-receiver in the living room, an upstate newspaper lying on the table—and by the bedroom door.

He had left that door open—and now it was closed!

Wentworth got a spare automatic from the desk, slipped a clip into it, and then snapped out the living-room light. Warily, he took hold of the bedroom doorknob, turned it softly and inched the door open. The room was dark. His questing fingers found the switch, pressed it. When he pushed the door wide, he found a counterpart of himself asleep in bed—*Terry Trimble himself!*

Of course, Trimble simply had come home from the Adirondacks and gone to bed. Wentworth grinned at his own elaborate precautions. Then the grin faded from his face, and he quickly leaned over the bed and put his hand on the still face.

Terry Trimble wasn't asleep—he was dead! He had died in his sleep… and on the wall facing him was a framed etching of Death's bony, beckoning hand!

Feeling as if he were looking down at his own corpse, Wentworth backed away from the bed and examined the room with hard, cold eyes. Nothing seemed to be out of the ordinary, except a shallow pan on the floor a short distance from the head of the bed. He picked it up and discovered the faintest vestige of sediment in it.

That pan had evidently contained some sort of liquid which had evaporated. His thoughts flashed to the poison-gas executions performed in some of the Western states. A few pellets of concentrated chemicals dropped into an acid solution could kill....

Now he began to understand how the Sleeping Death operated!

The gas, generated from that pan, slipped into the room when Terry Trimble was asleep, must have suffocated him instantly—even before he had a chance to raise his head from the pillow.

Bitter rage surged into Wentworth's heart, as he visualized that cowardly murder. Poor Trimble had not had a chance. He gazed down at the still features, realizing what Trimble's death meant to him. Now Richard Wentworth was doubly dead!

CHAPTER 9
DOCTOR OF DISASTER

SOLEMNLY, WENTWORTH pledged revenge to that innocent victim who had died in his stead. This was another murder for which the criminal fiend behind the Sleeping Death would pay to the full, he vowed as he turned away furiously.

But who was that monster? It must be Anderson. Wentworth had *seen* him in the Calvin Memorial, leading his killers—and yet how could Anderson have managed to get that pan of death into the locked apartment? Also, if it was Anderson, the man must have known the murderous attempt had failed when he saw Wentworth alive in the hospital. Or was the cunning devil now chuckling over Wentworth's escape, secure in the knowledge that the unsuspecting victim was going home to his death?

The answer to those perplexing questions lay with Emil Anderson. The truth would show plainly in his expression the moment he found himself face to face with his supposed victim. Terry Trimble must not be dead—yet. His death must be kept quiet, the body hidden, until Wentworth had had time to confound and expose his killers.

In the living room was a large closet. Lifting the corpse from the bed, he carried it there, stretched it out on the floor, then locked the door. That finished, and a pair of automatics holstered beneath his armpits, Wentworth was ready to interview Dr. Anderson....

It was long past midnight when he dismissed his cab and walked up the Fleming Hospital steps, but his ring brought a prompt answer. Dr. Anderson himself opened the door and stood back to let him enter. Wentworth's keen eyes could detect not the least start of surprise, or the slightest hint of guilt, in the physician's manner. Almost, it was as if Anderson had been expecting him.

Unquestioningly, he led the way to his office and offered Wentworth a chair beside his desk. He listened calmly as Wentworth voiced his suspicions, leading up to the events in the Calvin Memorial.

"You didn't know it, Anderson," Wentworth flung at him, "but you passed within six inches of me as you went through that autopsy room. I was beneath a sheet on one of the tables. I saw you—*and heard every word that you said!*"

Anderson nodded. There was a worried frown on his face, but no fear or uneasiness.

Dr. Anderson was tightly
bound at wrists and ankles…
then Wentworth was next.

"I have not left this building all night," he said in a matter-of-fact tone. "You do not have to take my word for that. I can prove it by my assistants and nurses. At the time you mention, I believe the record will show that I was in consultation with Doctor Coman, an outside physician who has placed one of

his patients with us. However," he admitted, "I confess that I expected something like this to happen. For some time I have been discovering various things which have led to a definite conviction. Somebody is *impersonating* me—obviously, for no good purpose."

He went on. "Consider this, Mr. Trimble. If I were the cunning murderer you practically accuse me of being, do you suppose I would go running around giving myself away at every turn so that I could not fail to be recognized? Obviously, not. I am surprised that whoever is responsible for this situation has been so crude about it. From what you tell me, I am now convinced that someone has been using my personality to cover up his own mischief. Someone doing everything possible to plant the guilt for his crimes on me!"

Pushing back his chair, he opened a drawer of his desk. He took out a sheaf of papers and handed them to Wentworth—more than a dozen prints of the beckoning-hand etching!

"I found these yesterday, tucked away in the bottom drawer of this desk, under a file which I very seldom use." He nodded as he saw Wentworth's surprise. "That is only one thing which aroused my suspicions. There have been others. Articles of clothing disappeared—particularly my shoes—stationery and other articles that have vanished from my desk. There have also been telephone calls—from men who seem to think that I have information about matters of which I know nothing. At first, I was skeptical. Now I am certain that I am being victimized."

"Why didn't you go to the police—especially when you found those etchings in your desk?" Wentworth wanted to know.

"Because, my dear Mr. Trimble—" Anderson seemed trying hard to remain patient—"I haven't the slightest idea of the identity of my impersonator. If I could name him and have him arrested, that would be a simple matter. But I can't. Going to the police would only involve me in difficulties and result in a great deal of undesirable publicity for the hospital."

His hands clasped and unclasped continually, his feet tapping the floor nervously as he leaned forward to stress his words. Wentworth had to admit that the argument was logical. Nevertheless, even though Dr. Anderson seemed genuine m his earnest disavowal, Wentworth could take no chances.

"Your story sounds straight, Doctor," he admitted. "But after what I have seen, I need more than your word to accept it. I want to search this building from top to bottom—and you're going with me."

As he spoke, his hand reached into his coat, came out gripping one of the automatics. "Sorry," he apologized, as the gun muzzle centered on Anderson, "but, you will understand, I can't afford to take chances."

The physician's dark eyes widened as he stared into the menacing barrel; his lips parted as if to voice a protest. Then he seemed to think better of it, shrugged and pushed back his chair.

"Whatever you wish," he agreed as he led the way.

ROOM AFTER room, they toured the four-story building. Uncomplainingly, Anderson opened every door, answered every question. Nothing whatever seemed to be suspicious or significant—until they reached the laboratory. It was dark. Anderson switched on the light and stood beside Wentworth in the doorway.

"Our dietitians and laboratory assistants finish their day at six o'clock," he explained, and his hand again reached toward the switch.

But Wentworth's alert eyes had spied a small door at one side of the room, almost concealed by a large case.

"That door—" He nodded to it. "Suppose we have a look at that, Doctor." And this time he sensed at once that he had stumbled onto something of importance.

Anderson's face flushed and, for a moment, he seemed on the point of refusing. Then his shoulders sagged and his eyes had the look of one who resigns himself to the inevitable. Without a word, he led the way across the laboratory, opened the door to reveal a smaller laboratory adjoining the main one—a work room in which George Holden was busily engaged in the midst of an array of bottles and experimental apparatus!

Holden whirled at the intrusion, half-rose from his stool, and then he sank back, white, haggard.

"You've got me," he said doggedly. "I knew you'd catch up with me, sooner or later. You've got me," his voice rose passionately, "but your cleverness will mean the doom of this city! You're playing right into the hands of the murdering thieves who are throttling it! Take me, cart me off to jail! But remember that I warned you—the responsibility is yours!"

He walked halfway to where Wentworth stood covering him with the gun—then his defiance died. His face worked spasmodically, under the stress of his emotions.

"I know what you think," he muttered. "I know how things look against me—as if I were guilty as hell. That's why the police are hunting for me. But I'm as innocent of this fearful thing as you are. The fault is partly mine, I admit that. But it was none of my doing, and I've done the best I could to repair the damage for which I am partly responsible. I've been working every minute that you fellows would let me—trying my best to develop a counteracting formula—"

"Easy," Wentworth interrupted his passionate flow of words. "Take it easy so that I can make out what you're trying to say."

"You know most of it anyway." Holden got hold of himself and became more coherent. "It is my formula that is the basis for this Sleeping Death. I was at work on poison-gas research for the War Department—working here in my private laboratory— when my notes, my almost complete formula, disappeared. I blamed it on the clean-up woman, and she was discharged. But when this terrible Sleeping Death scourge began, I knew that my work had been stolen and fallen into the hands of crimi- nals—into the hands of someone who had completed it and made a hellish murder weapon of it."

He continued. "I didn't dare go to the police, because I knew that I would be jailed. Someone called me on the telephone a week ago and warned me that I would be framed, if I tried that. They had my papers and it would have been easy to plant the guilt on me. To make doubly sure, they made it look as if I had killed Gene Fajans—which made me a fugitive. Don't you see," he pleaded, "my only hope of combatting this frightful menace lies in finding an antidote, a counteracting formula—something which can be distributed broadcast, so as to nullify the effects of the destroyer. That's what I have been working at night and day, trying to do—working whenever you fellows haven't been hounding me!"

"Have you any suspicion who stole the formula?" Wentworth asked.

"I don't know…" The pathologist hesitated. "I can't prove a thing, but I suspected Willis Fleming. Various things made me fairly certain that the formula was in *his* safe when he died—in fact, I thought that he might have been killed by those who wanted to get it. That was why Miss Cahill went to his apartment. She got a bundle of notes and memoranda from the safe, but before she had a chance to bring them to me they were stolen from her."

"How about Doctor Anderson?" Wentworth shot at him suddenly. "Has it ever occurred to you that he had access to this room—that he might be the one who took your formula?"

"Doctor Anderson? He has been working with me, striving as hard as I to develop a counteracting gas!" Holden came to the superintendent's defense at once. "It was Doctor Anderson who located me in the Kenilworth Arms and brought me materials so that I could work while the police were hunting for me. It was he who saved me and got me safely out when thieves raided the apartment. I *know* that Doctor Anderson isn't the guilty one—because I was escaping from the apartment with him when I saw a man, who looked just like him, leading the thieves into my rooms!"

"A man who looked just like him?" Wentworth followed up

quickly. "What do you mean by that? A man you would have taken for Doctor Anderson if you had not been with him?"

"Yes." Holden did not hesitate. "A very clever impersonation—in fact, I even caught a glimpse of the acid scar on his hand."

THE YOUNG pathologist's story sounded convincing, and his apparent sincerity was infectious. But there was no way to check up on his claims at that moment—and the peril, in case he was lying, was too great. Nita's danger, and the menace that hung over the whole city, was too appalling to take any chances with this man. Wentworth did not feel justified in letting him run loose. Holden belonged in custody, confined somewhere so that, guilty or innocent, he could do no more harm.

That meant turning him over to the police, to Stanley Kirkpatrick—and taking the police commissioner into Wentworth's confidence, letting him know that the friend he thought buried was still alive. But that must be done—Wentworth's duty to the city's helpless millions demanded it....

"I can't let you stay here, Holden," he said firmly. "I am going to hand you over to the police. My word has some weight in the department, and I think I can assure you that, on my recommendation, you will be given every opportunity to go on with your work. But you will have to do it under guard so that there will be no possible chance for you to—"

The moment he announced his intention of calling the police, Wentworth saw the wild alarm in Holden's eyes. The man's hands trembled as he backed up against his work table... but now something hard pressed against the small of Wentworth's back.

"Don't try to turn and grab my gun," Doretta Cahill's tense voice warned him. "I'll shoot, if you do."

No blustering threat—just the grim, flat-voiced warning of a desperate woman who would do exactly what she promised. Wentworth made no attempt to test her nerve.

"Drop your gun on the floor," came from behind him. He could feel the weapon against his ribs quiver, as her finger tightened on the trigger. "Kick it over into the corner."

He obeyed—and Holden was quick to take advantage of his release. The moment the gun muzzle no longer covered him, he leaped from his stool and threw himself on Dr. Anderson, bore the man backward to the floor and overpowered him—with what seemed to Wentworth suspicious ease.

Running to a closet at one side of the room, Holden came back with a bolt of heavy hempen twine. Quickly, he wrapped the tough cord around and around Anderson's ankles; then drew the superintendent's hands behind his back and secured his wrists. Wentworth was next. Helplessly, he stood there while his hands were lashed together behind his back, then forced to lie on the floor as his ankles were secured....

Wentworth was battling with those lashings, even before Holden and the girl were out of the laboratory. But the knots were tight and he could little more than twist his wrists one against the other. Anderson seemed to be having better luck. There was more play in his bonds and he could slip one hand halfway up to the other elbow. All of this took time.

"Roll over here and turn your back to mine," Wentworth told him. "I can work on those knots better than you can."

Back to back, they lay on the floor while Wentworth's cramped fingers tugged away at Anderson's wrists. It did not take long. The loosely woven hemp frayed easily, and he soon had the knots untied so that the physician could twist one arm free, then complete the job himself. As soon as he was untied, he did the same service for Wentworth.

"I'm sorry about this, Mr. Trimble," he apologized as he worked. "Perhaps I should have told you about Holden, but I did not want to see him arrested. I had full confidence in him—and even now I attribute his behavior to panic rather than guilt."

The man seemed entirely sincere. But when he left the hospital Wentworth admitted to himself that he was totally at sea. Either the doctor was an innocent man or an exceedingly clever crook, and the same held for George Holden and Doretta Cahill....

CHAPTER 10
EYE FOR AN EYE

IT HAD been Jenkyns, the butler, who answered the telephone in Richard Wentworth's Sutton Place home the terrible night the police called to notify the household of Wentworth's death. The old man's face had blanched and his hand trembled as he held the instrument to his ear.

"Dead?" He repeated the frightful word. "You are... certain?"

"Not much doubt about it," the harsh voice on the wire

clipped. "He was riding in a car with Miss Nita van Sloan. She is in the Calvin Memorial Hospital. Wentworth's body was pretty badly mangled, but there is plenty to identify him. That's why I'm calling. We want someone from his home to come down and complete the identification."

Jackson had taken the instrument out of the old man's hand before that announcement was finished. "I'll be down immediately," he agreed, and then turned to where Jenkyns had sunk into a chair.

Ram Singh had suddenly materialized out of nowhere. "The master," the Sikh gasped intuitively, "he has been injured—seriously?"

"They say he's dead," Jackson said slowly, as if he were surprised at the words that were coming from his own lips. "Killed in an automobile accident. But—" he determinedly took hold of himself—"we have heard news like that before and found it to be... somewhat exaggerated. I'm taking no stock in this rumor until I've seen the body with my own eyes!"

Vigorously, they agreed with him, but as they looked into each other's eyes they each knew that they were afraid. There had been plenty of rumors and reports of Wentworth's death in his eventful career. Somehow, this was different. Each of them sensed it, felt the chill touch of calamity at the back of his neck....

That visit to the morgue had been a heart-rending ordeal for Jackson. When he looked down at the horribly mangled remains, a pain that was white-hot stabbed through him... and left him weak and sick. The infernal machine which had wrecked the car must have landed right on the driver's lap...

What was left of the face seemed to be Wentworth's—though, Jackson admitted, it could have been anyone's else as well. But the card-case, wallet, cigarette case, ring—there was no doubt whatever about them.

On their evidence he completed the identification. Yet as he rode back to Sutton Place, the whole thing seemed a nightmare. Wentworth dead... that couldn't be! Wentworth *couldn't* be dead. There must be some other explanation—*had* to be! That body simply could not have been Wentworth's. By the time he got back to Jenkyns and Ram Singh, he was sure of it—and they were all too ready to be convinced.

Hopefully, they waited all that night and the next day, one of them always posted beside the telephone, certain that Wentworth would call. But the phone remained silent. All day Jackson scouted around town, tried every source of information. Wentworth had been seen nowhere. He had disappeared completely—"disappeared," because Jackson still would not admit that he could be dead.

Then Jackson remembered Blinky McQuade! Wentworth had disappeared before, sometimes for days; and during those times Blinky McQuade had roamed the underworld. That was the answer! For some reason of his own, Wentworth wanted to slip into his McQuade character. To locate the cowardly devil who had nearly killed Nita—that was the reason! Jackson tried hard to make himself believe that. To check up on it, he and Jenkyns took up their vigil at both entrances to the Holian Alley tenement, while Ram Singh stayed close beside the telephone.

For two nights and a day they alternated on that watch, but

there was no sign of Wentworth. Finally, desperate for confirmation of some sort, Jackson broke into Blinky McQuade's room, and had to admit that there was no evidence that it had been occupied for weeks....

"The major seems to be... gone," he reluctantly admitted that night when the three were gathered in the Sutton Place living room. "There seems to be nothing else to believe. But, for the present, we are going on just as if he were still here with us. That is what he would have wanted us to do—until Miss van Sloan is recovered and ready to take charge."

The next morning was the funeral service, for which Jackson had made all arrangements, even while trying to convince himself that the body to be interred was not that of Richard Wentworth. Alert for trouble from the bomb-throwing murderer of his henchmen, Jackson and Ram Singh were eagle-eyed during the simple service at the funeral chapel. But by the time the cortege had reached the cemetery, and the casket was being lowered into the grave, their vigilance had somewhat relaxed. Then came the attack which almost cost Jackson his life.

"Without the master, we are as children!" Ram Singh heaped reproach on himself as he reached Jackson's side and helped him to his feet after the gangsters' car had roared down the cemetery road.

"Maybe we're children, Ram Singh," Jackson panted, "but somebody else in this graveyard isn't a child. Who shot those killers out from under my nose? Whoever did certainly saved my bacon."

"I did not see," the Sikh confessed contritely. "Like a baby I had tripped and fallen on the ground."

"Probably some guard that Commissioner Kirkpatrick had posted around the plot," Jackson decided. But later, when he made inquiry, Kirkpatrick disavowed any guards, and nobody had identified the mysterious sharpshooter... a fact which was mulled over and over again in Jackson's puzzled mind.

HE WAS still speculating on it the next afternoon when a caller rang the bell of Wentworth's apartment in the building that faced on Sutton Place. Leaving the stronghold on the water's edge that was Wentworth's real headquarters, Jackson hurried to the apartment by means of the underground tunnel which connected the two. When he answered the door, a woman stood in the hallway—a woman probably in her middle fifties, well preserved and still showing the traces of what once probably had been far more than average beauty.

"I am Jessie Ogilvie," she introduced herself, as Jackson tried to tell her of Wentworth's demise. "I know that Mr. Wentworth is dead—that's why I am here. I want to talk to his men, to his friends—to someone who is interested in bringing his murderer to justice."

Jackson ushered her into the apartment and introduced himself, sat opposite her and studied her shrewdly as she resumed.

"You are just the person I wanted to meet, Mr. Jackson." She nodded her head vigorously, and he could see the vengeful flare in her eyes. "You were devoted to Mr. Wentworth and want to see that his murderer is punished, and I... Well, Willis Fleming

119

His guns were beating a deadly tattoo—a steady blast

of death against which no man could live!

was my son. He was murdered, Mr. Jackson—murdered in the most cowardly fashion by those he trusted. I will not rest until they get what is coming to them!

"They think they will get away with that murder, but they won't, Mr. Jackson." She leaned forward, put her hand on his knee, and he could feel the trembling tension of her body. "I have sworn that they won't. I have been working constantly to avenge him—working with Sylvia Lane. She was Willis'—er—sweetheart. Sylvia has discovered who they are—they are the same ones who murdered Mr. Wentworth!"

Triumphantly, she sat back and watched him. She saw the grim white line of his mouth, the hard muscles that bunched at the ends of his jaws.

"This is no case for the law, Mr. Jackson." Her voice was low and hard. "It is one thing to know that a murder has been committed and another to prove it to a jury. These men have money; they can hire the best criminal attorneys. They will talk or buy themselves into the clear—and probably have me killed for attempting to have them prosecuted. I want to avenge my boy! I can't do it alone—I need help. That's why I have come to you. I have heard that Mr. Wentworth's men adored him, that they would do anything for him."

"But how are we to know that these people killed Mr. Wentworth?" Jackson was skeptical. "You say they did, but we would have to have more than that before we could consider doing anything—"

"Of course," she agreed quickly. "I expected that—and I have a plan by which you can convince yourselves. It will make these murderers confess—they will give themselves away and, at the same time, be at the mercy of you and your friends. Sylvia Lane has worked her way into their confidence. She is supposed to be the sweetheart of one of them, and so she knows all their plans. If you will help me, we can trap them tonight."

Swiftly, she rushed on, outlining her plan step by step. As he listened, Jackson's fists clenched. The plan was daring—the sort Wentworth would have liked. It ought to work. If she was right and these men were the ones who had murdered Richard Wentworth, this would drive them into the open. That was all that Jackson asked....

WENTWORTH'S SLEEP was a thing of fits and starts the night he returned from the Fleming Hospital. All night he seemed to be running around in circles and getting nowhere. He told himself that, the next morning when he tried to lay out a course of action for the day.

Action was what he wanted—he was on edge for it but did not know where to turn. Every trail followed so far had only led him into a blind alley; every clue had petered out or wound up in a baffling question mark. Every angle had been investigated and... yielded nothing.

One by one, he checked them off. The Morellis, Doc Roth, Dr. Sanderson, George Holden, Doretta Cahill, Sylvia Lane, Sam Pavvy, Hammer Gunther... There was still one he had not followed up—the woman who had been with Gunther that night outside Willis Fleming's apartment....

Who she was, Wentworth didn't know, but she might have been Gunther's partner, Jessie Ogilvie. Jessie Ogilvie—who might also have been the Jessie whom Hulbert Fleming had mentioned as he was coming to his senses... Somewhere, Wentworth was convinced, Jessie Ogilvie fitted into this puzzling picture—both she and Hammer Gunther. Their connection with it might be the string that would unravel the whole tangle.

He already had discovered that Jessie Ogilvie had been a popular actress some three decades ago, and now he decided to find out more about her. The public library might be a good place to start.

As soon as he had called Dr. Rogers and ascertained that Nita was resting comfortably and showing marked improvement, Wentworth started on his quest. Old magazines and books on the stage, he pored through by the dozens—not only in the library, but, after that, in the dusty racks of a second-hand bookstore famous for its stock of old newspapers and magazines.

Deep into the past he delved, and gradually, out of those musty archives, two lives began to reshape themselves—those of Jessica Ogilvie and Hulbert Fleming. Jessica Ogilvie, one of the prettiest women on the stage and the toast of the nightlife of her day; and Hulbert Fleming, scion of an old, aristocratic New York family.

Young Fleming, it appeared, had been very much enamored of the fair Jessica. There were accounts of parties he had given for her, social functions to which he had taken her in defiance of raised eyebrows, and then there were hints of a coming marriage—but at that point his parents had whisked him off to Europe for a year.

Shortly after his return, his engagement to Marguerite

Debevoise, a young woman of his own social set, had been announced. His wife had died several years later, leaving no children; and a few years after that Hulbert had adopted the four-year-old Willis.

By this time, Jessica Ogilvie had faded out of public notice. For some reason, she had retired from the stage, and her name dropped out of the newspapers almost entirely. In a few years, she had been forgotten by all except one society reporter who printed the rumor that she had given birth to a son in some Western city.

In those old illustrated magazines Wentworth found several photographs of Jessica Ogilvie in her prime, and instantly he was struck with her resemblance to Willis Fleming....

It was evening before he had finished his research. When he contacted Dr. Rogers at the hospital he learned that the physician had been anxiously trying to reach him for several hours.

"No, it isn't Nita." He set Wentworth's instant fear at rest. "She is doing very nicely. It's your men in Sutton Place who have me worried. I was talking to Jackson this afternoon and learned that they have worked out a plan to avenge your death. I tried to soft-pedal it, of course, but that didn't click. They are very sure they can trap your murderers. The thing is scheduled for tonight—for about nine o'clock, so far as I could make out."

Wentworth didn't wait to hear any more. Slamming the telephone into its cradle, he bolted out of the apartment for the nearest taxi. Nine o'clock... That meant that they might have left already, but with luck he would still arrive in time to head them off.

RAPIDLY, HE made his plans as the cab sped uptown, endeavoring to figure out what Jackson and Ram Singh intended. Who were they going to try to trap—the Morellis? If he were certain that was the answer, he might be tempted to let them go ahead. He could trail them and take a hand in the game himself once the killers were located. But he couldn't risk this. In their eagerness to avenge him, his loyal friends might annihilate some innocent suspects. Or they might....

He must head them off—

But he was too late for that! Just as the taxicab swung into Sutton Place, a car whisked out of the side-street entrance to Wentworth's grounds and sped past. He caught only a fleeting glimpse of the driver, but Ram Singh's turban was unmistakable.

"Never mind stopping," he quickly redirected the cabbie. "Follow that car. Not too close—I don't want them to know they're being trailed."

Across town the course led, all the way over to Ninth Avenue, then up to Sixty-sixth Street. Ram Singh parked at the curb halfway to Tenth Avenue, and Wentworth paid off his cab at the next corner. By the time he had walked back, his men were at the foot of the elevated station, Ram Singh, Jenkyns—and a counterpart of Wentworth himself!

That was Jackson, of course—but what could be his idea? On a mission of vengeance he was playing the role of the corpse itself!

Suddenly Wentworth began to understand, and quickly changed his plan. Instead of interfering or divulging his identity, he would trail along with them and stay in the background, but ready to take a hand when his assistance was needed.

From a nearby doorway, he watched them go up the stairs to the station and then followed at a discreet distance. With his face buried in a newspaper he had picked up at the downstairs newsstand, he passed them on the platform, sauntered slowly to the north end and then, when he was certain that he was unobserved, swung over the railing and down onto the catwalk beside the tracks.

There, safe from the eyes of anyone at the station, he set to work with his makeup kit, transforming the features of Terry Trimble into the ugly mask of the Spider. Before the first train rolled into the station he was crouching low on the catwalk, the black hat pulled low over his glittering eyes, cape wrapped around him so that he seemed only a deeper patch of black in the surrounding darkness.

The three on the station platform let that train go by, and the one that followed it, but boarded the third—a Sixth Avenue local. Wentworth caught hold of the chains at its rear and drew himself up onto the back platform. Crouching on the floor, he peered through the window.

There were at least half a dozen men in the rear car whom he readily labeled gangsters—hard-looking, shifty-eyed individuals who appeared on the alert, hair-triggered for something which, he could see, must be scheduled to break very soon. At Fifty-ninth Street a dozen more came in—with them the two Morellis, dark eyes darting up and down the car and flashing with approval!

Straight to the center cross-seats they walked, while their fellows, Wentworth noticed, ranged themselves along the right side of the car and left the other side empty, except for a few uneasy passengers. Tense and watchful, Tony Morelli stood up and supervised their alignment, shifting them here and there like a football quarterback making certain that his men were all in position before calling the signals.

Satisfied at last, Tony turned to resume his seat—then suddenly his swarthy face drained of all color, became a dirty yellow-gray. His eyeballs seemed to swell out of his head; his heavy jaw dropped open. Then a shriek of wild, superstitious terror broke from his parted lips as he clawed frantically inside his coat!

Turning toward the front of the car, Tony's astounded eyes had beheld something that could not be! The front door had opened—and in stalked a dead man! There, before him, stood Richard Wentworth, whose body had been torn to pieces by an infernal machine, whose corpse had been riddled from end to end by machine-gun bullets! That was what he saw now.

"No—no!" Horrified protests slobbered from his lips as he backed away. He jammed up against the seat in his fearful anxiety to keep as much distance as possible between himself and that incredible thing from the grave. "*Esta della Madonna*—keep him away from me!"

AT THAT moment the train was rounding the corner of Sixth Avenue and Fifty-third Street. All but the last car had completed the curve when the brakes went on and the cars bumped together as they came to a stop. As if that unseating jolt was the signal, pandemonium broke loose—a bedlam of smashing glass and thundering guns.

But Tony Morelli did not see his fellows smashing out the windowpanes with their gun muzzles, or the machine guns nosing through the broken windows to blast a leaden hail into the second-floor windows of the corner building that was almost within hand's reach. He saw only that unholy figure walking inexorably toward him.

"So you *did* kill him!" Jackson's voice was as cold and relentless as a death sentence. "You murdered him without giving him a chance!"

That right hand that had been empty now held a gun, pointing straight at Tony Morelli. Tony's trembling fingers were tugging his own weapon from the holster. But it slipped out of his wet grip, clattering to the floor.

"*Sapristi!*" he howled in utter panic.

Then the death sentence was executed. Jackson's gun roared, and a bullet hole sprouted in the center of Morelli's forehead. Another tunneled through his heart. For a moment he tottered crazily on rubbery legs, then crashed down on top of his brother.

With a howl of rage, Vic Morelli sprang to his feet and his bellow warned his fellows of this new danger at their rear. Instantly, they whirled. The car became a madhouse—a den of savage, murder-mad beasts, eager to blast out of existence those three grim-faced executioners backed against the front door, slavering to tear them limb from limb!

"Get them!" Vic screamed. "The dirty sons—"

His obscene epithet ended in a strangling gurgle, as Ram

Singh's bullets shattered his jaw and ripped through his throat. Deliberately, the tall Sikh fired, without the slightest change of expression on his impassive, bearded face. Beside him Jackson's gun poured death into that snarling pack. From behind, where they had pushed him to protect him as much as possible with their own bodies, old Jenkyns picked his men and made every bullet count.

But the odds against them were overwhelming. It could be but a matter of moments before they were borne down, trampled underfoot by those rapacious killers. Already the glass behind them was shot to pieces, the car-frame pockmarked with bullet holes. Blood was soaking Jackson's collar and the front of his shirt, and Ram Singh's left arm hung useless at his side. Only a matter of moments now....

On the back platform, the Spider was frantic! Not until he tried to open the door and rush to their rescue had he discovered that the guard had locked it!

Desperately, he hammered at the glass with his automatic butt, shattered it and beat the sharp shards out of the frame so that he could grab hold of the sides and hoist himself up—to leap into the car like the creature from which he had taken his name... a great black spider scurrying out from the vortex of its web!

Guns blazing, hideous face contorted into a terrifying snarl, his eerie howl rising above the infernal bedlam, the Spider took those gun-brave thugs completely by surprise. For a fraction of a second, there was a lull in the riotous uproar while the startled killers turned to locate this fresh menace, a split-second of near quiet—and then a howl of livid fear.

"That's the Spider!" one of the tommy-gunners shouted, and hurled himself headfirst through the window, only to be caught midway by one of the Spider's bullets.

Frantic lead whipped at the Spider, but his crouching figure was mercurial. Darting from side to side of the blood-spattered car, his guns were beating a deadly tattoo, a steady blast of certain death against which no man could expect to stand.

Jackson and Ram Singh were brushed aside, pushed back on top of Jenkyns by that frenzied stampede. The door behind them was flung wide, clotted with fleeing thugs, when suddenly a terrific blast went off directly beneath them—a peal of man-made thunder that dwarfed the best of nature's awesome efforts!

The earth seemed to tremble and quake, with the shock of that ear-splitting explosion. The death-ravaged car appeared to rise in the air dizzily, while terrified men clutched at anything for a handhold—and then it plunged downward sickeningly when part of the steel elevated structure buckled and crumpled!

Steel girders, twisted rails and wooden ties rained down on that car as it crashed with stunning force on the sidewalk, upended and, like a great fish out of water, slapped its rear platform against the crumbling front of the corner building before it thudded, upside-down, onto the street!

DAZED, ALMOST blinded by the explosion and the stupefying crash as the car hit the street, Wentworth squirmed his way out of the tangled mass of struggling men now packed

131

into the front end of the wrecked car. Clawing his way up toward the middle, he caught hold of the cross-seats in the center, crawled in behind them and paused for a moment's respite. Subconsciously, his fingers went to work, stripping off the cape, hat and wig, obliterating as far as possible the telltale ugliness of the Spider.

Wentworth started back toward the squirming heap. Jackson, Ram Singh and Jenkyns were somewhere in that human sardine-pack—perhaps pinned down helplessly!

Then he saw the Sikh's turban in one of the windows. Ram Singh was lifting out an unconscious body that must be Jenkyns, as Jackson clambered out after him onto the sidewalk. Wentworth was free to go now. Dizzily, hand over face, he staggered up as he climbed through one of the shattered windows. He blundered, apparently blindly, into the gaping crowd.

His blindness was only feigned. Between his fingers, his alert eyes were missing nothing, probing every face, watching every move. He recognized nearly a score of those faces—the jubilant, well satisfied faces of underworld denizens who had taken part in the Music Hall battle. They were minions of the master of the Sleeping Death!

And there, among them, was the fiendish monster himself! No doubt about it now.

Grinning evilly in the front rank of the milling crowd stood Dr. Emil Anderson, chuckling over what undoubtedly was his handiwork! Dr. Anderson… or an impersonator who was his double!

Red rage seethed in Wentworth's brain, but there was nothing he could do at that moment. His own disguise had duped him. He was hog-tied, faced with the necessity of escaping before he should be picked up by the police and identified as the Spider. Helplessly, he turned away and dived through the crowd, started up the avenue until he spied a taxi.

"Get moving—fast," Wentworth snapped, as he gave an address several blocks from Trimble's apartment.

The Morellis and their gang had walked blindly into a trap... a trap no doubt baited by the master of the Sleeping Death. Those second-story windows that the killers had deluged with lead—no doubt they belonged to one of the headquarters of the devilish "chief." No doubt those who should have been behind them were fully prepared and waiting for the attack.

It was a cleverly baited death-trap, and into it, with the intended victims, had walked the Spider and his avengers....

CHAPTER 11
WANTED FOR MURDER!

AS THE taxi bore him across town, Wentworth's skillful fingers removed what was left of the Spider's repulsive visage and restored the features of Terry Trimble. So thorough was that transformation that the driver gaped at him unbelievingly when he got out and double-paid his fare. He gaped, and then started up his machine, probably to report to the first policeman he met....

It was to forestall such an attempt that Wentworth had not driven directly to the apartment house. Now, when he approached the building, he silently thanked his lucky star for that inspiration. Halfway down the block, he saw that something was the matter. A crowd had blocked the sidewalk.

As he came nearer, he saw that an ambulance and three radio cars were drawn up at the curb.

Instantly, he froze, backed away unobtrusively and mingled with the crowd until he could watch without fear of being seen. Now there was a stir in the doorway. The police were moving aside, opening a lane for two white-uniformed stretcher-bearers whose burden was covered from end to end by a sheet—a corpse on its way to the morgue!

It was Terry Trimble's corpse!

Wentworth was as sure of this fact as if he had seen beneath the sheet. A moment later, he was positive. After the stretcher-bearers came Commissioner Kirkpatrick and the medical examiner. Stanley Kirkpatrick's florid face was even more saturnine than usual, the first knuckle of his right hand worriedly brushing his spiked mustache. Only a murder, and an important one at that, would have brought the police commissioner here.

Somehow, Terry Trimble's body had been discovered in that locked living-room closet. The killers must have notified the police, sent them there to search the place and discover their handiwork. No matter what else it accomplished, Wentworth realized that their cunning maneuver had closed the Trimble apartment to him as a haven. It had shorn him of the Trimble disguise, as well. Now every detective in the city would be quick to recognize and pick up either Terry Trimble or Richard Wentworth, two men supposed to be dead!

Wentworth must get rid of his makeup at once.

Three blocks away he found a barroom, slipped in through the side door and walked to the washroom before the bartenders had a chance to get a look at him. In one of the toilet compartments, he went to work—and the disguise that had served him so well disappeared for the last time.

When he stepped out again and stopped at the bar for a drink, he appeared to be an inconspicuous-looking man of middle age.

"We interrupt our program to bring you a special bulletin from the press radio bureau," the radio on the back-bar announced. "The police of New York City tonight uncovered a remarkably audacious case of impersonation and murder in discovering the corpse of Terry Trimble, a private detective, who was killed in his own apartment and then made the victim of an impersonation while his corpse was locked in a closet right in his own rooms.

"A sensational development in the case is the murder warrant which has been issued for the arrest of Richard Wentworth, well-known society man, who was supposedly killed in a bomb explosion on Monday night and buried on Wednesday. Police Commissioner Kirkpatrick announced that he had conclusive proof that Wentworth was not killed in the bombing and that he has been impersonating Trimble and living in Trimble's apartment since his supposed death.

"Trimble, it has been discovered, was vacationing in the Adirondacks until yesterday afternoon, when he returned to his apartment and met his death. Even after Trimble's death, Wentworth continued the masquerade and lived in the apartment with the murdered man's body. Besides charging him with Trimble's murder, the police are arranging to exhume the body which was buried as Wentworth's, to determine its identity and investigate whether or not it also was a victim of murder."

There it was. He was wanted for murder—the murder of Terry Trimble!

GRIMLY WENTWORTH listened to those fantastic charges. He had not been mistaken in thinking that he was recognized in the hospital when he stripped off his Trimble makeup for Nita's benefit. There *had* been a woman outside that door. She had recognized him and promptly relayed her discovery to the master of the Sleeping Death.

But who was the woman who had done this?

Sylvia Lane, probably. Her connection with the murder chieftain was definitely established. Yet it might easily have been Doretta Cahill. She might have waited for him outside the Kenilworth Arms, trailing him home to the Trimble apartment and from there to the hospital. The eavesdropper might even have been Jessie Ogilvie, taking a renewed interest in his affairs....

Perhaps Dr. Rogers had caught a glimpse of that woman? Wentworth had not thought to ask him. Now he went to a telephone booth in the bar's back room.

"No, I didn't see a woman at Nita's door," Rogers answered. "And I can't recall noticing a woman in the corridor that night. But speaking of women, Jackson mentioned several when he told me about his plan for avenging you. There was a Miss Ogilvie—Jessie Ogilvie—who called at your home and interested them in the scheme. She wanted to enlist their aid to avenge her son. Then there was another woman—Sylvia Lane, I believe was her name—who was working with her. As I understood it, Sylvia Lane had secured the information for the Ogilvie woman."

Jessie Ogilvie, as he had suspected, was Willis Fleming's mother. Rabid to avenge his death, she probably had listened eagerly when Sylvia Lane claimed to know the identity of his killers. She had gone to enlist the aid of Wentworth's men. That probably was also at the suggestion of Sylvia Lane, he suspected—might even have been suggested to her on direct orders of the "chief."

So it was Sylvia Lane who had tipped off Jessie Ogilvie where to contact the Morellis! The Morellis were part of the chief's organization, and no doubt they were the ones directly responsible for Willis Fleming's death. To that extent Sylvia Lane's tip had been straight. But evidently the Morellis had gotten out of control. Apparently, they were trying to take over the racket, or at least were reaching out for the spoils themselves—and for that had been put on the spot.

With consummate guile, the master of the Sleeping Death had schemed to rid himself of his own troublemakers, and also Wentworth's loyal followers, who might prove troublesome if not eliminated. Sylvia Lane had been his go-between, Jessie Ogilvie his catspaw....

The ruthless scoundrel could sit back and laugh, Wentworth conceded bitterly, as he summed up his own failure. The Morellis and Doc Roth were dead; Hammer Gunther was dead, and the Ogilvie woman had disappeared; Sam Pavvy was dead, and

George Holden and Doretta Cahill had vanished. Dr. Anderson, despite the damning appearance against him, apparently was in the clear. Nowhere was there a tangible clue for Wentworth to follow... even were he not a fugitive from justice!

And meanwhile the poisonous terror of the Sleeping Death was spreading into every home in the city!

THE MIDNIGHT editions of the morning papers, which Wentworth took with him when he checked in under an assumed name at a third-rate hotel, featured the usual tabulation of Sleeping Death victims and accounts of lawless atrocities attributed to the scourge. Even the outrage of the dynamited elevated train bore the sinister stamp of the dread destroyer when firemen, putting out the blaze in the wrecked cars, found an etching of the beckoning hand nailed up in his booth beside the murdered motorman!

But it was not until morning that the terrified metropolis staggered back from a full realization of its own helplessness—a brazen announcement and ultimatum from the master of the Sleeping Death himself!

It appeared on the front page of one of the city's most widely circulated papers.

Wentworth stared at that humbled, desecrated journal, and the outrageous edict fairly leaped out at him, flaunting itself before his eyes—

THE SLEEPING TAX
TO THE CITIZENS OF NEW YORK CITY:
It is my intention to be entirely fair in the assessments I am

imposing on this city. I want the burden to be no heavier on one than on another. For that reason I have decided to levy a "sleeping tax" on every dwelling in the same manner as the city levies a real-estate tax. Within the next few days, every owner of a habitation will receive his bill. Payment will be made promptly when my agent demands it—or the Sleeping Death will be the alternative.

Furthermore, to assure my agents freedom from molestation, I warn that under no circumstances are they to be attacked, detained, or in any manner interfered with, in the performance of their duties.

Finally, I demand that all attempts to apprehend or interfere with me must cease—and give warning that any further police activity directed at me or my organization will result in reprisals against the citizens of the city.

THE SLEEPING DEATH

That disgraceful screed was a contemptuous insult to every red-blooded man in the city. What could have possessed the publisher to open the columns of his paper to such a bullying threat and insidious attack upon the already panic-stricken public?

But Wentworth knew the answers to those indignant questions. Wheeler adored his wife, idolized his two daughters and had reveled in becoming a grandfather. Wheeler knew that the police could not protect his loved ones.

Even before he ventured from the hotel that morning, Wentworth was prepared for what he would encounter—but the effect of that brazen proclamation was even more far-reaching and paralyzing to the city than he had anticipated.

It was evident on every side, wherever he turned.

Only one topic was on every tongue—the outrageous demand of the master of the Sleeping Death. Only one thought in every mind… how to pay or how to escape the inevitable penalty.…

THE STREETS were crowded with people, many of whom had been out all night, daring to catch a few winks of sleep only in the parks. Mass claustrophobia had descended on the city, as terrified men and women refused to go into the buildings where they should have been at work. They did not dare stay in their own homes. Only outside could there be safety.

Men and women with haggard, fear-lined faces; men and women who plodded along hopelessly, going they knew not where; men and women with wild, unseeing eyes and twitching, nonsense-babbling lips; men and women asleep in doorways, against newsstands and house fronts, wherever they might have been when exhaustion overtook them—on every side Wentworth saw the pitiful ravages of days and nights of unremitting terror.

New York had become a shuddering city of fear that dared not sleep! All who could do so were fleeing. Taxis stood at the curbs, gathering customers for distant points—Long Island, New Jersey, Connecticut, wherever there was a promise of refuge and sleep.

When Wentworth got back to midtown and reached the Grand Central Station it was a swarming maëlstrom of anxious-eyed, terror-stricken humanity. From every direction people seemed to be converging on it.

For hours he shoved and squirmed his way through that densely packed throng, his great heart torn with anguish for these innocent sufferers, his tireless eyes watching and searching… for a face that he felt certain he would find. It would be a grinning, evilly triumphant face, gloating over this unparalleled horror.

Slowly, he began to work his way to the Forty-second Street entrance. Before he was halfway to the door, the whole building seemed to tremble with the reverberation of a mighty clap of thunder. In through the doors swept a blast of cold, wet air that was a boon in the hot, humanity-packed station… and then, from outside came the sound of rain.

Fleeing before the deluge, hundreds of people, who had been aimlessly roaming the streets, now swarmed into the station. Pressed forward by additional hundreds at their rear, they jammed the corridors, surging into the main auditorium that already seemed filled beyond capacity.

Caught in that human flood, Wentworth was carried back into the big room he had just left, swept back into the middle of the press. By the time he managed to brace himself and hold his ground, he was almost within reach of the information booth that rose like a lighthouse over that sea of worried faces.

For a moment he stood there, eyeing the close-packed station, trying to figure the best chance of getting out of it… and in that moment all hell seemed to break loose!

At a dozen points the crowded balconies suddenly began to

clear as the thundering rattle of pistol shots rang out above the din of excitedly chattering voices. At a dozen points men and women went down, screaming horribly, or threw themselves wildly over the railing onto the heads of those below.

Immediately, those little clearings were filled—by gas-masked men who cradled submachine guns under their arms. Guns that covered the frantically milling crowd, cleared the balconies and stairs, forcing those who had been standing on them down into the hysterical mob below. Those watchful gunners were followed by other gas-masked figures with tanks that looked like large-sized fire extinguishers strapped onto their backs. Hose nozzles were in their hands.

"The doors are locked!" The fearful discovery sped from mouth to mouth. "There are machine guns at the doors! We can't get out! We're trapped!"

It unleashed a roaring flood of mad panic. Blindly men and women beat and tore at one another. Screaming wildly, they fought to climb over the bodies of their neighbors. Up from the frightful turmoil rose a blast of sound that might have escaped from the pit of hell itself—an ear-splitting roar of mad terror.

And down upon it hosed death from the spraying nozzles attached to those tanks on the balconies!

The moment Wentworth had glimpsed those gas-masked devils he knew what to expect. When the doors closed, he knew that the great station was being made as airtight as possible. Now he had scant minutes in which to work if he was to prevent the most ghastly mass slaughter in civilized history....

FIGHTING HIS way to the information booth now

142

deserted by its terror-stricken crew, Wentworth leaped over the counter and crouched on the floor behind it. From beneath his coat came the gas mask with which he had equipped himself at his hideout garage. As soon as it was in place over his face, it was topped with a floppy-brimmed black hat… and over his shoulders went the midnight cape of the Spider.

Down from those balconies poured the Sleeping Death! Streams of invisible, colorless gas destroyed the very air, clutched at men's throats and closed their eyes in everlasting sleep! And there, in the center of one of the walls, was an immense reproduction of the fatal beckoning hand, projected from a stereopticon!

Death beckoning to those helpless, close-packed thousands!

"I gave this city fair warning," a harsh voice rasped out over an amplifier. "Your police have disobeyed me—and this is my answer!"

Hardly had the last strident syllable echoed boomingly through the dome than it was followed by a weird howl, a shivery cackle of maniacal laughter—and the Spider leaped to his feet, perched on the edge of the booth top like a great vulture. Then he leaped down into the maelstrom!

It did not seem that that packed crowd could jam together any more closely, but the sight of that awesome creature leaping down on top of them worked a miracle. Men pressed backward frantically, flattened themselves against one another, and a way opened for him….

So quickly did he move that he was almost to the foot of the balcony stairs before the machine-gunners fully grasped what was happening. Before their leaden hail could more than graze him he had leaped to the staircase, darted up crazily, weaving from side to side like a dancing phantom, while his blazing guns picked off the tommy-gunners with unerring aim.

Three of them reared upright and slumped to the floor—and then the Spider was over the foremost, tearing the deadly "type-writer" from his nerveless fingers. Holding the fellow's corpse in front of him as a shield, he gripped the weapon and turned its death stream on the masked fiends all around him.

The unholy terror the Spider's reputation had long since inspired in the heart of crimedom—that flaming gun in his hands, dealing out to them the death they had expected to serve only to others—drove those masked killers back. The sight of their falling comrades unnerved them, and suddenly they broke in utter panic—broke and started to flee just as a raging madman came up in their rear.

Two of them the newcomer shot down mercilessly before he stemmed the tide and rallied the others. With blazing gun he led their charge, a familiar-looking figure even beneath the gas mask....

Wentworth glanced at this man's shoes, at the carriage of his sloped shoulders—and he was sure of his identity. Deliberately, with grim satisfaction, he swung his chattering weapon and seamed that mask with lead.

The leader went down....

His fall completed the rout momentarily checked by his arrival. Pell-mell those gas-masked killers turned and fled, just as Wentworth reached the still quivering body and yanked the mask from the dead leader's face. As he expected, he stared down at features that could belong to none but Dr. Emil Anderson. The mouth, nose, eyes, high forehead—all were natural features without a trace of makeup. Even the acid-scarred right hand was there!

Quickly, Wentworth slipped his own hand into his vest pocket, brought it out again gripping a little cigarette lighter. For a moment he pressed the bottom of the metal contraption against the forehead of the corpse—and where it had rested was a crimson replica of a spider! A warning to the underworld, high and low, that, even though the police might be flouted, he who would build an empire of crime sooner or later must reckon with the Spider!

"They're running!" he shouted down to the frenzied thousands below. "Now is your chance to wipe them out before they have a chance to reorganize! If you value your lives, follow me!"

A score of the bravest and most desperate led the way. Others flocked after them, stormed up the steps, snatched up the guns the dead killers had dropped. But before they could follow up the momentary advantage Wentworth had gained, the killers were coming back, tommy guns clearing the way as they regained their ground almost to the balcony.

Wentworth's machine gun was empty—but at that moment he spied a weapon even more deadly than the lead-spouting "chopper." It was one of those tanks filled with Sleeping Death! Crouching over one of the dead thugs, he swiftly unstrapped the tank, fastened it over his own shoulders—and turned the hose nozzle onto the rallied thugs as his automatic blazed at their masks.

Even with the protection of their masks, the killers quailed before Wentworth's death bath. At such close quarters they wanted nothing to do with the Spider but backed away fearfully—then took to their heels in earnest. In mad flight they raced from the station while the Spider, the death tank discarded, led a charge that finally reached the doors and broke the siege.

The station had been saved. But scores of bodies littered the balcony and stairway, and hundreds on the floor below had succumbed to the effects of the gas.

Diving into the still terrified crowd, Wentworth stripped off his cape and hat and discarded them as he plunged into the work of rescue. Now the police had arrived and managed to clear part of the congested station. Ambulances had been summoned, and white-uniformed interns were relaying loaded stretchers to them.

"Give me a hand with this woman," Wentworth called to a reporter, as he started to pick up an elderly woman who was retching and gasping for breath. "We can get her out to an ambulance before they have time to pick her up."

"Not enough ambulances out there, that's the trouble," the reporter swore softly as he gave willing assistance. "Of all the low-down deviltry, incapacitating the hospitals before an outrage like this is the rottenest."

"Incapacitating the hospitals?" Wentworth asked… and a cold chill of premonition ran down his spine.

"I just heard about the Calvin Memorial," the news-hawk

told him. "From what I could hear, the whole place was wiped out. Sleeping Death, of course. You'll notice there are no Calvin ambulances outside."

The Calvin Memorial—Nita's hospital—stricken! The Calvin Memorial had been wiped out!

Wentworth hardly heard what the reporter said after that, or knew what he was doing as he lifted the moaning woman into an ambulance. All that he could see was Nita's face in front of him… Nita's dead face!

The moment he was rid of his burden, he dived into the crowd that clogged Forty-second Street from side to side. Endlessly, he seemed to be wriggling and shoving, twisting and fighting his way through them, until at last he reached Madison Avenue and was able to hail a cab.

Arriving at the hospital, he leaped out and raced for the entrance. He dashed through the police cordon, gained the doorway—sprinting across the corridor and up the stairs to her private room. He flung open the door—and stared at an empty bed.

Nita was gone!

From room to room he roamed, seeking her everywhere, anywhere. But all that greeted him was death. Like the guests at the Kenilworth Arms, the patients in the Calvin Memorial Hospital had died in their beds, in their chairs, in the midst of whatever they were doing.

Most of the victims were still in their rooms just as they had died, but some others had been gathered together and stretched out in long rows in the corridors. Down those pitiful lines Wentworth walked, dreading at any moment that he would find Nita beneath the next sheet.

But she was not there. From top to bottom he searched the hospital, but nowhere could he find a trace of her. Back in her empty room, he studied the bare walls as if he would wring from them the secret of what had happened to her… and suddenly his gaze stopped, fastened on the ventilator.

There was something peculiar about it… And then he realized the truth. That ventilator was closed up tight, and those in the other rooms were open. To check up, he went next door, then into half a dozen more rooms, to all in that wing of the building. Every ventilator was open. Nita's, alone, was closed—and Nita, alone, had disappeared. Nita might have lived through that deluge of death.

Suddenly, Wentworth was certain of it. He recalled those dark figures on the roof of the Kenilworth Arms—and knew why they had been there. They had sent the Sleeping Death into every room in the hotel *through the ventilators!* That was how Holden's apartment had been spared—his ventilators must have been purposely closed, exactly as Nita's had been. The death which flowed into the other rooms did not reach hers. She had been saved from that—saved for God only knew what horrible fate!

CHAPTER 12
THIRD AND LAST DEATH

B UT *who* had saved Nita and taken her away from the
hospital? *Who* was this fiend who warred on the sick and
helpless?

It could not be Dr. Anderson, he told himself. Emil Anderson now lay dead in the Grand Central Station, even though
Wentworth had not been able to locate his trampled body after
the thugs were routed. Also, from what he had learned of the
time of this attack on the hospital, Anderson could hardly have
been on the scene of both crimes.

But if it wasn't Anderson....

One by one, he checked off every possible suspect in the
entire case, no matter how remote their connection. He had
investigated all, and cleared them. It could have been none of
them, except... And then he had the lead he had been seeking!

Hulbert Fleming!

It was Fleming who had fathered Jessie Ogilvie's boy—then
adopted him. It was his crooks who killed Willis Fleming rather
than let him squeal to Wentworth. That was what old Hulbert
had meant when he muttered Jessie's name as he came back to
consciousness—it was also she who had threatened to kill him
to avenge her son.

Bit by bit, the pieces began to fall into place. By that time,
Wentworth already had hailed a cab and was speeding to the
Fleming mansion.

The more he considered it, the clearer the muddled situation became. Sylvia Lane, Willis Fleming's mistress, was really a hireling of the elder Fleming's—or else she had gone over to the old man as soon as Willis was killed. That was why she had been waiting there in the penthouse the night after his death—waiting to spy on anyone who might come to investigate Willis' affairs. Then she would report to Hulbert. That, of course, was how he had learned the identity of Sam Pavvy and Hammer Gunther... and then put them both on the spot in the Yankee Music Hall.

Hulbert Fleming was the real master of the Sleeping Death, and had been using Emil Anderson as a tool, a cover-up!

Would Fleming be at home? Had he taken Nita there, to hold her a prisoner on his own premises? Wentworth had no way of knowing—but the mansion must be his first destination.

Grim-lipped, narrow-eyed, he left the cab and strode toward the front steps of the mid-Victorian mansion. Then common sense whispered in his ear, checked his rage. If Hulbert Fleming was the master of the Sleeping Death, it would be sheer suicide to walk up to his front door.

Wentworth studied the place from across the street, front and side—and *there* was the way!

Patiently, Wentworth watched until the street was entirely empty. Then he walked across the street, went up the side steps and paused for a moment at the top as if about to ring the bell. There was not a sound in the building; nobody came to see what he wanted. He dropped over the stair rail into the little recess beside the bay window.

Out from beneath his coat, unwound from around his waist,

came a length of sturdy silken rope—a strand of the Spider's web that had more than once proved his salvation. Fastening a wide loop in one end, he tossed it overhead. On the second attempt, it settled over the metal ball surmounting one of the balcony posts.

Making sure once more that he was not observed, even though his position was almost entirely hidden from the street, Wentworth went up that line hand over fist.

Cautiously, he tried the window that opened onto the balcony. It was locked, but his glass cutter made short work of that problem. Reaching inside through the hole it carved, he turned the knob and stepped through the French window into a bedroom. The bedroom was unoccupied. Silently he cat-footed into the upper hallway, stopped and listened. Not a sound came to him.

When he had reached the lower floor that impression seemed substantiated. One after the other, he tiptoed through the big rooms and found them empty. Not a soul; not a sound… until he froze and listened. The indistinct rumble of a human voice was coming from somewhere below him!

In a few moments, he located the stairs that led down to the basement, descending warily on the creaking steps. It was dark down there in the basement hallway, and he did not dare risk a light. Slowly, he groped his way along toward the rear—and caught himself just in time to avoid tumbling headlong over something huddled in the middle of the floor. It was something soft and yielding, that fairly made his foot and leg tingle….

Bending over it, Wentworth's hand touched a human body—a woman. Still closer, shielding its pencil ray with his coat, he turned his pocket flashlight on the gruesome find…

the dead face of Jessie Ogilvie! Jessie Ogilvie, brutally murdered, clothing soaked with the crimson torrent from her crushed and battered skull!

Jessie Ogilvie, it seemed, had tried once too often to avenge her murdered son....

Again Wentworth caught the sound of a man's voice.

Stepping over the blood-spattered corpse, he stalked farther toward the rear of the house, until the corridor turned at right-angles and led to a partly open door some fifteen feet away. Creeping up to this, he nudged it gently, pushed it back until he could see into one end of the lighted room beyond.

The room was a laboratory; a completely equipped workroom which Hulbert Fleming had installed for Willis' use when he lived at home.

Crouching close against the wall, Wentworth maneuvered into a position from which he could see nearly half of the interior. His fingers clamped tight around the butt of his automatic. *There, lying on a hospital bed, was Nita!*

HER FACE was almost as white as the sheet that covered her. A pallid mask, out of which great, dark eyes stared, tensely watching something that was taking place in front of her. Nita, so weak that she could only lie there, a helpless prisoner at the mercy of this murdering devil!

His voice was coming louder.

"She was a drain, a constant source of expense to me," the voice said. "She depleted my fortune and forced me to look elsewhere for money to meet her constant demands. That is why I conceived the plan of the Sleeping Death. For her part in this

I killed her, when she came here tonight. The others who had a share in this monstrous scheme shall suffer likewise when I have finished this statement. George Holden, because he perfected the death gas for me; Doretta Cahill, because she assisted him and helped administer it to victims; Nita van Sloan…."

Hulbert Fleming repenting—yielding to remorse! What sort of hollow mockery was this?

Wentworth crept forward until he was halfway through the doorway. The laboratory was within his range of vision, and now he saw that it was not Hulbert Fleming who was voicing that conscience-stricken confession. Fleming was sitting at a table, cowed and trembling, obediently writing down the words being dictated by a black-robed, hood-masked figure.

That figure was the "chief" to whom Sylvia Lane had taken him. Now, as then, Wentworth eyed the fellow critically and saw that his resemblance to Emil Anderson was unmistakable. As an impersonation, the performance was perfect—but didn't the man know that his masquerade was a joke? Didn't he know that Emil Anderson was dead?

Wentworth had thoroughly convinced himself that the chief was Hulbert Fleming, but this astounding development completely upset his theory. Now he was at a loss even to guess at the identity of the man beneath the black robe. Once more, the master of the Sleeping Death had outwitted him. But this time cunning could do him no good.

"Nita van Sloan—" the voice that was so much like Emil Anderson's, but *couldn't* be, went on dictating—"because she and Richard Wentworth were two of my trusted lieutenants until they tried to kill me and grab the Sleeping Death organization for themselves."

That astonishing lie was more than Nita could stand.

"No!" she gasped weakly, as she propped herself up on the bed. "Don't write that—it isn't true! I won't let you!"

Before they knew what she intended, she had gotten her feet down onto the floor, staggered uncertainly toward Fleming and grabbed for his pen and paper. Shaking with terror, Fleming's eyes flashed up to hers appealingly—then glued once more to the table, when the black-robed chief lashed out with his arm and brutally flung her back onto the bed.

Blood trickled from the corner of Nita's mouth, and a sob moaned up from her lips. That sob stabbed into Richard Wentworth's brain like a red-hot, searing iron and drove him utterly berserk. Like a wild man he sprang into that room.

The chief whirled just in time to make a frantic grab for Wentworth's gun-wrist—to drag it to his masked face and sink his teeth into it!

Wentworth's grip on the gun broke as those teeth sank into his flesh. The weapon dropped to the floor, and a spasm of pain shot through the whole length of his arm. Fiercely, he hammered at the cowled head with his free hand, pounded down at it and smashed his fist into the masked face. That gained him a momentary respite. The bestial grip on his wrist was broken as the black-robed fiend cursed and staggered drunkenly backward.

Instantly, Wentworth was after him, lashing punishing blows into his stomach until he doubled up with pain—then snatching at the cowl-mask. Frantically, the fellow tried to back away, to jerk his head out of reach. But Wentworth's clutching fingers hooked into the edge of the mask and clung to it, ripped it from top to bottom so that it tore away—revealing the snarling, murderous-eyed face of Dr. Emil Anderson!

WENTWORTH HAD been more weakened than he realized by the superficial wounds he sustained in the Grand Central Station battle. The few moments of this struggle now made his head spin.

He had killed this man once—and would do it again! He would kill the fiend a hundred times, if that was necessary.

He hurled himself at the fellow, pistoned his fists into the snarling face and drove Anderson back, back, until he was up against a stationary table and could go no farther. Like one of his caveman ancestors, Wentworth swarmed over the mass murderer, snapping his head back with an uppercut to the jaw— then sinking steely fingers into the muscles of his throat. His hold tightened like a vise.

"The pity is that you can only die once," Wentworth gritted down at him, "for Earl Saunders, Terry Trimble—"

Suddenly, his words stopped, his punishing fingers held where they were, and he half-whirled toward the laboratory doorway. Out there in the hallway pandemonium had broken loose. A shrill shriek of terror echoed through the room, and then the sounds of a savage tussle, a woman's voice begging and pleading, screaming in horror. Into the room ran Sylvia Lane, her dress a tattered ruin.

Like a trapped animal she cowered in the middle of the room, covering her half-naked breasts with her arms—then she flung herself onto Wentworth.

"Stop him!" she begged. "You *must* stop him! He'll kill me if you let him take me! Please—"

Her hands gripped his shoulders, slid around his neck and held him tightly as her arms wound around him. Like a leech she clung to him, forcing herself between him and Anderson. The physician broke clear, staggered back and gasped for air.

Instantly, he returned to the attack, while Wentworth fought to free himself from the woman. Anderson's fists lashed out, smashed Wentworth's face, again and again, dazing him, pounding him backward out of the girl's grip, following up triumphantly, to knock him to the floor and then meet him with a crushing blow from a swung chair the moment he climbed groggily to his knees.

Half-conscious, head spinning dizzily, senses reeling, Wentworth tried to shove up to his knees... then crumpled to the floor under Anderson's kicking heels.

"Very well done, my dear," the physician panted at Sylvia Lane, as he turned away from Wentworth's prostrate form. "You would make an excellent actress—if there was any occasion for you to work for a living."

Picking up the automatic which had dropped from Wentworth's hand, Anderson stepped back to the table and grinned down at Fleming. The old man still sat, ashen-faced, holding the pen.

"I think that about finishes it," Anderson chuckled. "That covers all the fool questions the police will ask. Now for a concluding paragraph. Take this. 'When this statement is discovered I shall have paid in full for my crimes. As a final expiation, it seems only fitting that I and all those associated with me in directing the criminal organization I built up, should yield our lives to the Sleeping Death. Signed—Hulbert Fleming, Dispenser of the Sleeping Death.'"

FROM WHERE he lay on the floor, slumped against a cabinet table, Wentworth dazedly saw the rest of the laboratory—the opposite side, where George Holden and Doretta Cahill lay tied hand and foot. The girl's eyes followed Dr. Anderson's every move. Her eyes were brimming with terror and loathing, but Holden hardly seemed aware of what was going on around him.

Wentworth saw how they would all die. In the center of the floor a large basin had been set—a basin which could be there for only one purpose....

"That's right, Wentworth," Anderson caught his eye and nodded confirmation. "You've guessed it. That's the flowing bowl where we'll mix up enough chemicals to fill this laboratory with sufficient death for a hundred people. I rather expected you to show up here today. It saves me the trouble of going after you—to make you pay for murdering my brother, Edgar, when you played the gallant hero in the Grand Central a few hours ago."

His brother! In a flash of understanding, Anderson's ruse was clear to Wentworth! Emil and Edgar Anderson had been twins—*identical* twins.

Taking advantage of the fact that Edgar's existence was unknown even to Hulbert Fleming and his other associates, Emil had concocted his devilish scheme. The master of the

Sleeping Death would seem to be Dr. Emil Anderson but could not be he, because he would always be at the hospital or somewhere else where he could be identified when his brother was seen under compromising circumstances.

Deliberately, he had let himself or Edgar be seen from time to time in the enactment of their crimes—using the very boldness of that maneuver as an alibi, evidence that he must be the victim of a criminal impersonation. Carefully, he had planned to throw the blame onto Hulbert Fleming, to have the old man accused of masquerading as him in order to make it appear that Anderson was the guilty party....

"I should have thought of a twin brother," Wentworth admitted, the words coming painfully from his stiff lips. "There really was no other possible explanation. But you covered it very cleverly, Anderson—even reproducing the acid burn on your brother's hand."

Anderson grinned appreciatively and opened a cabinet at one side of the room, removing three large frosted-glass bottles.

"You and Fleming were in the thing together, of course," Wentworth rushed on, desperate to hold the fellow's attention for a few minutes more. "But you planned to double-cross him from the start—to grab everything for yourself and throw the guilt onto Fleming when the cream of the loot had been taken."

"As it is now," Anderson smirked. "I am no hog. I know when it is time to call it quits."

Clever, diabolically clever, Wentworth had to concede. With Fleming dead and blamed for the Sleeping Death, Anderson and Sylvia Lane—who, it was now clear, had been working with him from the start, tricking both Hulbert Fleming and Willis—would be perfectly safe. As soon as the furor had subsided, Anderson would resign his job and they would slip away to enjoy their tremendous fortune.

"We don't want to have our friends waiting here too long before they are discovered." Anderson laughed mockingly as he stood looking around at his captives. "Suppose you call the police, Sylvia? Get Commissioner Kirkpatrick, if you can—I believe he is a particular friend of Wentworth's and is extremely anxious to see him. Tell them that you just saw Wentworth entering the Fleming mansion. That should bring them in a hurry—just in time to break in on the last victims of the Sleeping Death!"

Gladly Sylvia Lane complied. Wentworth heard her heels clicking down the hall, heard her dialing a number—and then her voice summoning the police, who would find only dead bodies when they arrived....

Mustering every ounce of his depleted strength, he got to his knees, to his feet, flung himself desperately at that grinning murderer. But Anderson's gun butt caught him on the jaw, smashed him back to the floor. Deliberately, Anderson emptied one of those bottles into the basin, then added the contents of another.

"Dick... Dick, darling," Nita whispered a farewell.

"Enjoy yourselves, my friends!" Anderson jeered... and the contents of the third bottle joined the other two in the basin! Yes, this was undoubtedly the end!

Grinning mockingly, the devil-doctor backed quickly toward the door, reached for the knob to draw it shut—and then tensed, his face suddenly frozen, his ears straining, listening unbelievingly. Out there, somewhere in the hall, a wild confusion had broken loose—shouts, the pounding of running feet, the sounds of a scuffle, and then Sylvia Lane's voice shrieking in mingled rage and fright.

"Emil—look out!" she screamed.

After her leaped three gas-masked figures and a white streak that sped through the doorway like a bullet—three grotesque-looking creatures led by one who wore a *turban* over his gargoyle mask!

RAM SINGH took in the situation at a glance. He dived headlong, threw himself to the floor and covered the basin with his body so that its deadly fumes had no further chance to spread. At the same instant, the broad-shouldered figure, whom Wentworth would have recognized as Jackson no matter how his face was disguised, leaped at Anderson, grabbing him by the collar.

Like a wild man, Anderson fought to break loose. Scratching and clawing, he was utterly beside himself in his frenzy to get out of that laboratory before the death that he had meted out to so many others should catch up with him. The automatic which he had taken from Wentworth and dropped to the floor, in the sudden surprise of this invasion, had been momentarily forgotten in his mad terror. Now he saw it, dived for it.

The moment Anderson's fingers touched the weapon, a bullet from Jackson's steady gun bored right through his skull... Turning quickly, Jackson ran to where Jenkyns stood over the figure of an aristocratic-faced old man slumped over a porcelain-topped table. Jenkyns, his automatic trained on the gray-haired head, was shaking the man's shoulder… but that ready weapon was no longer necessary. Hulbert Fleming had gone through too much excitement. Half-paralyzed with fear for the past hour, his weakened heart had stopped.

The Sleeping Death was at an end, its devilish authors fittingly punished… all except Sylvia Lane!

Her face an unlovely mask of rage and bitter disappointment, the girl who had been Emil Anderson's inspiration and co-plotter stood in the midst of her ruined hopes and ambitions. In a moment's time she had been plunged from the height of triumph, from wealth and power, down to utter defeat—with the grim specter of death beckoning her to the electric chair! She was utterly defeated and ruined—but at least that other woman would not live to glory over her! In a burst of uncontrollable rage, she ran across the room and threw herself upon Nita.

Ram Singh shouted a warning. Jackson whirled. But before any of them could reach her, a savage fury leaped, snarling, across the intervening space. Straight at Sylvia Lane's throat, Apollo's powerful jaws snapped shut and his sharp fangs sank deep in the flesh, crunching the bones of this creature who had tried to harm his beloved mistress….

WHILE JENKYNS helped Wentworth to his feet, Jackson quickly bent over Doretta Cahill and George Holden, liberated them both. His servants were now watching Wentworth with awe, reverence.

"The police will be here at any moment now," Wentworth said, taking charge. "I can't stay to meet them. Miss van Sloan must be gotten away at once. But I want you to stay, Holden— you and Miss Cahill. You know the whole story. You have seen everything that happened—and now you are in the clear. You can make the explanations for the rest of us."

"There is very little time, master," Ram Singh warned from his position on the floor, when the moment of silence had passed. "The police...."

Jackson already had lifted Nita in his arms, and Jenkyns was gently helping to steady Wentworth, as they went out into the corridor. They passed through a side basement door to where Wentworth's familiar big Daimler stood at the curb. Police cars were already sirening down the street as Ram Singh, the last of the party, leaped in and closed the door.

Like a torpedo, the Daimler shot away from the curb, flashed by the oncoming cars and sped uptown. Tense and narrow-eyed at the wheel, Jackson said not a word until he had effectually buried the car in traffic and pursuit was past.

"How did you do it, Jackson?" Wentworth asked at last. "How did you know where to find us?" He waited, smiling.

"Apollo," Jackson said, smiling now. "He's a better detective than any of us. He followed the car that took Miss van Sloan from the hospital, and then he came home to Sutton Place—just as if he knew he would find help there."

Wentworth's fingers reached down to the faithful Great Dane's head, patted it.

Apollo had seemed to know that he would find help at Sutton

Place… and as Wentworth's eyes turned from one to another of these loyal friends, the animal's wisdom rebuked him. There had been help for *him* at Sutton Place, too—help that he had not called upon because he had felt that he must wage his fight single-handed. Now he realized that there were situations that no man can meet alone. But for Jackson and the others, Nita would now be lying in that house of death….

Wentworth bent over her and pressed a kiss to her lips.

"Keep driving north, Jackson," he directed softly, as he saw that she had fallen asleep. "We are going out of the city."

For a long while, he silently promised her. The Spider had fulfilled his duty to his helpless fellows. Now Richard Wentworth was going to do his duty by the one who had suffered most for him—was going to lose himself for months in some quiet hideaway where he could woo her back to health and strength!